To Dina
with much
affection

Mr H.

THE MISSING CONCORDAT

A Tale of Suspense and Intrigue

By

NORMAN HUBLEY

PublishAmerica

Baltimore

Hardcover 9781630000264
Softcover 9781627097062
PUBLISHED BY PUBLISHAMERICA, LLLP
www.publishamerica.com
Baltimore

Printed in the United States of America

This book is dedicated to my grandchildren
Stephanie, Erica, Noah, Matthew,
Grace, Michael, Daniel, Caroline,
Jane, William, Priscilla, Ann, Gavin,
&
Angela Joy Hubley
(Aug 19, 1978 - Feb 2, 1997)
—taken from us so young

PROLOGUE

November 1975 . . .

Only one more packet of papers remained to be examined. Like all the others, it was neatly tied with the pale yellow ribbon bearing the official seal of the Jefatura Del Estado. The Monsignor reached behind his head and unbuttoned his clerical collar. The room was stuffy and he had been smoking too many cigarettes. He pushed his chair away from the table, stood up, and walked to the window. Through the dust-covered pane, he could see only a fire escape and the brick wall of another building. He tried to open the window but it was sealed shut and he could not budge it. He gave up trying, brushed the dirt off his hands, and lit another cigarette. He sat down again at the table.

The door to the small room in which he was sitting opened. He turned and saw the two soldiers of the Guardia Civil still standing outside, machine guns slung over their shoulders. They snapped to attention and saluted as a gray haired man in a drab military uniform strode briskly between them into the room. "Excuse me for interrupting you, Monsignor Grappi, but you have been at this task of yours for several hours. I thought you might wish to have something to eat."

The Monsignor declined. "That is very kind of you, General, but I am almost finished and prefer to wait. I appreciate your thoughtfulness."

"A glass of sherry, perhaps?"

"No, thank you, not just now." He glanced toward the window. "I do not suppose you could open that for me; the room is rather close."

The general shook his head. "I am sorry but the window cannot be opened; it has been sealed shut for a number of years." He apologized. "It is too bad you have to work here under such uncomfortable circumstances. But the Generalissimo's testament was quite specific that his papers were to be examined here in this very room where they were kept."

The Monsignor nodded. "I understand. It is all right; I do not have much more to do." He paused. "When I am finished, I would very much like to have that glass of sherry."

The general bowed and left the room.

The Monsignor untied the last packet of papers. They appeared to be just more of the same: old letters, faded photographs, personal memorabilia, nothing that could not as easily have been examined by any bureaucrat in the government. Why someone thought it necessary that a representative of the Holy See examine them in private, he did not understand. But it was not his place to question the matter. His instructions had come directly from Cardinal Borielli, the Vatican's Minister of Finance, one of the most powerful men in Rome. And the instructions had been clear. He would be the first person to see the papers after Franco's death, a week ago. He was to examine them carefully in the manner the Generalissimo had specified in his will, without anyone else present. Then he was to return to Rome and report to Cardinal Borielli, and to no one else. He smiled to himself. Only a few more documents remained to be examined. If they were like all the others, his report to the Cardinal would be brief and uninteresting.

He glanced at the next piece of paper. He was about to throw it on top of the others when something caught his eye. He drew heavily on his cigarette. The piece of paper had been *torn from the last page of some formal agreement entered into at the Vatican on March 26, 1941. He searched through the remaining papers but the agreement itself was not there. He looked again at the torn piece in his hand. Beneath the Jurat and the date were the signatures of the two men who had signed the missing document. His cigarette began to burn his fingers. He crushed it out but did not take his eyes off the two signatures. He recognized both. The one on the left was the finely scratched signature of Pope Pius XII. The other, written in heavy black letters, was that of Adolph Hitler.*

February 1941 . . .

In February 1941, Hitler made a brief visit, unrecorded by history, to Arromache au Bains, a small French town on the English Channel. Traveling in an unmarked car, accompanied only by his chauffer, he arrived early in the morning before the town was awake. He was driven directly to the beach. He told his chauffer to remain in the car and walked alone down to the edge of the water.

For several minutes he stood staring out into the fog. He was pleased with himself. In little more than a year, he had conquered virtually all of Europe and, as he promised in Mein Kampf, finally settled Germany's long score with France. His Wehrmacht had destroyed the British army at Dunkirk, and the Luftwaffer would soon finish off what was left of England's air force. His generals, Rundstedt, Rommel, and Guderian were waiting for the order to move their Panzers to the coast. Not in a thousand years, since William the Conqueror, had anyone stood as poised to plant a hostile foot on English soil. He continued to stare out into the fog for several more minutes. Then abruptly, he turned and walked back to his car.

The next day, in Berlin, he summoned his top military advisors to the Chancellery. To their astonishment, he announced that he was postponing any invasion of England, and that they were to begin preparations for Operation Barbarossa, the all out assault on Russia.

September, October 1978 . . .

Thirty-seven years later, on September 28, 1978, Albino Luciani was found dead. Sitting up in bed, still wearing his glasses, it appeared he was the victim of a massive heart attack. The news of his death flashed around the world. Only thirty-three days before, enjoying perfect health, he had been elected Pope of the Holy Roman Catholic Church. Chosen by the liberals in the Curia to continue the unfinished ecumenicalism of Pope John XXIII, his death now left in doubt what direction the Church would take.

Eighteen days after Luciani's death, the College of Cardinals elected his successor, Karol Cardinal Wojtyla of Krakow, Poland, the first non-Italian to ascend the throne of the Holy See in more than five hundred years. Wojtyla, who took the name John Paul II, was an arch-conservative.

The Vatican, March 1941 . . .

The velvet -lined elevator rose slowly to the third floor of the Vatican. Its sole occupant, a young priest, was puzzled. He had been roused from a sound sleep and summoned to the Pope's private apartment, told only that he was to bring his pen, a bottle of ink and a supply of blank parchment. He glanced at his watch; it was 2:00 a.m.

The elevator reached the third floor and the door opened. He stepped out and found the waiting room outside the Pope's office brightly lighted. Two men were standing in the center of it. He recognized one as Cardinal Tardini, the Vatican's Secretary of State. The other he had never seen before, a short gnomish-looking man wearing a gray business suit. Pinned in one of his lapels was a small black and white swastika. Tardini turned and smiled. "Ah, Father Borielli." He pointed to the Pope's office. "Go right in; His Holiness is waiting." Borielli tapped lightly on the white door, opened it and entered. Pope Pius XII was sitting at his library table. He appeared at first to be alone, but he was not. Someone else was there, a man standing by the window. Borielli's eyes widened. It was the Chancellor of Germany, Adolph Hitler.

The Pope motioned Borielli to join him at the table. "Thank you for coming so promptly, Father." He waited until Borielli was seated and then continued. "I am entering into an agreement I wish to have memorialized in a concordat. It is to be written in both Latin and German. I have chosen you to write it because I am told you are fluent in both languages and have a gift for flawless script." He leaned forward over the table. "But there is something you must understand. What you are going to be told to write is to be kept absolutely secret. After you leave, you are never to say anything to anyone about what transpired here tonight." He peered over his steel-rimmed glasses into Borielli's eyes. "Do you understand?"

Borielli nodded. "Yes, Your Holiness." He arranged his materials in front of him and waited.

Pius XII began dictating. Borielli wrote down the Pope's words first in Latin and then in German. After each sentence the Pope paused so Borielli could read back what he had written. Hitler listened carefully to the German, from time to time suggesting minor changes the Pope accepted without comment. The agreement was long and involved, the process painfully slow. Several hours passed and Borielli saw through the window that it was getting light outside. The table was now covered with the pages of his unique script. The Pope was getting weary. Hitler seemed tireless.

The arduous process continued, Borielli's pen scratching onto the parchment, word by word, the strange document he was being asked to create. He found it difficult to believe what he was writing. The document, a long rambling treatise, rationalized Hitler's territorial aggressions, portraying the German dictator as a man of vision who shared the Pope's concern that Christian Europe was threatened by atheistic Communism and international Zionism. In the concordat, the two men agreed that these threats must be eliminated.

The Pope dictated the next sentence. Borielli wrote it down in both languages and then read it back. Hitler asked to have the German repeated. Borielli had used the word "Ausrottung." Hitler wanted "Ausscheidung" substituted. Borielli hesitated. Hitler's word, while a synonym, could be interpreted literally to mean extermination. He looked at the Pope, uncertain whether to make an issue of the matter. Before he could decide, the Pope, now exhausted, began dictating again.

Finally, as the first rays of the sun sliced through the windows into the room, the Pope stopped. The document was finished. He waited while Borielli read back the final sentence, then signed the document and passed it to Hitler. Hitler signed his name beside the Pope's, and then stood up and walked back to the window. Pius XII took off his steel-rimmed glasses and placed them on the table. He looked at Borielli and managed a tired smile. "Thank you father that will be all."

After Borielli had left, neither Hitler nor the Pope said anything for several minutes. They were waiting for their next visitor. There was a knock on the door. It opened and the man they were expecting entered. Dressed in Mufti, he had come secretly from Madrid. The only man in the world they both trusted. He was Generalissimo Francisco Franco of Spain.

Madrid, May 1941 . . .

The crowd in the *Plaza de Toros* rose to its feet, everyone's eyes fixed on the battered wooden gate at the far side of the bullring. A trumpet sounded. The gate burst open and the last bull of the *corrida* charged out into the sun-drenched arena. It was a huge black Andalusian kicking up a trailing cloud of dust as it charged across the yellow sand, testing its powerful muscles. The crowd cheered. The bulls so far had all lacked courage and were poor kills. This one, everyone hoped would be different and provide a good *estocada.* The bull reached the center of the ring and stopped. It stood there, pawing the sand and moving its massive head slowly from side to side, looking puzzled.

High in the stands, seated next to the *Presidente de la Corrida*, his guest General Franco was also puzzled. All afternoon, while watching the bullfights and chatting with his host, his mind had been elsewhere. Three months had passed since his trip to the Vatican, and still he had not decided what to do with the document entrusted to him. Responsibility for its safekeeping weighted heavily on him.

He heard the crowd cheering again and glanced down in the arena. To everyone's delight, a *peone*, sent out to taunt the bull had barely escaped its horns as he scrambled to safety over the *barrera.*

Franco's thoughts returned to his problem. He had already decided that keeping the document with his other papers presented too great a risk of discovery. Yet it had to be retrievable in the event of his death. And it could not be entrusted to anyone else. The problem was a difficult one.

The trumpet sounded again. The final matador of the day stepped from the shade out into the brightness of the arena. The spangles on his tight costume caught the sunlight - and the attention of the bull.

Franco was not watching. He had closed his eyes and was concentrating. An idea had occurred to him and he was letting his mind massage it into a concrete plan. If he separated the document into two parts, he could then hide it in two different places. Neither part, if discovered, would reveal the full picture, yet the whole document would still be retrievable. He would tear off the portion bearing the signatures and keep it with his personal papers. The rest of the document he would entrust to someone else with instructions, if he died, to deliver it to the Vatican. Delivery of the signature portion he would handle by a provision in his will.

Shouts of *Ole!* rose from the crowd. The matador had just completed a series of graceful *veronicas*. Now, turning his back on the bull, he was strutting like a peacock to the *barrera*.

The trumpet sounded again. A *banderillo* danced out into the center of the ring to tease the bull and plant the razor-sharp *banderillas* in its neck. The *picadors* would be next and further wound the animal. Then the matador would return with the *muleta* and sword to perform the final act of the *faena*. Franco had seen it all hundreds of times. He closed his eyes again. He had almost solved his problem. All that remained now was to choose the person to whom he would entrust the other part of the document. His mind began screening candidates. It had to be someone from the past, he decided, someone he had never mentioned even to his closest confidants. He searched his mind for the right person: a Spaniard, of course, but one not living in Spain, yet not so distant as to make retrieval of the document difficult, someone who would accept it without question and safeguard it, not disclosing its existence to anyone. He continued to struggle with the problem, oblivious to the drama reaching its climax in the arena below. The bull, blood now streaming from its neck, lowered its deadly horns for the final charge. Only a few feet away, the matador stood poised, the *muleta* in one hand, the long thin sword in the other. As the crowd rose for the kill, the answer flashed into Franco's mind: the trip he took some years ago, hiking alone and incognito in the Italian mountains; he had forgotten all about it. Yes, that was the answer, he decided. He leaned back and smiled to himself. Yes, the person he had in mind would be perfect.

The crowd sat down, disappointed. The matador had missed his mark. The bull, the sword sticking awkwardly out of its neck, staggered toward the *barrera* and then collapsed to its knees, still trying to hold its head up. The *Presidente* rose, took out his white handkerchief, and signaled for the animal to be taken out of its misery gracelessly with the dagger-like *puntilla*.

***The Vatican, March 1977* . . .** Quiello Borielli, now a member of the College of Cardinals, closed his missal and placed it on the night table beside his bed. He turned off the light and lay back on his pillow in the darkness. He congratulated himself on what he had accomplished. Twenty-five years had passed since that fateful night when we was summoned to Pope Pius XII's private apartment and participated in the events he swore never to divulge. And since then he had not spoken a word about them to anyone. His silence had not gone unrewarded. Less than a year afterwards, he had been made a

Monsignor, the youngest in Vatican history. Other promotions followed, each subtlely arranged, advancing him steadily up the bureaucratic ladder of the Church's hierarchy, the latest, his appointment as Minister of Finance, one of the most powerful positions in the Holy See.

But none of this was why he was congratulating himself tonight. The reason was that, at long last, he had put together the strange puzzle that for years he had been trying to solve, the puzzle in which he was a small but intricate piece. The major pieces, Pope Pius XII, Hitler, and Franco, were all dead. But the picture now was clear. Hitler's plan had been a clever one. It might have changed the course of history. In 1940, he had conquered all of central Europe and stood poised at the English Channel. He did not fear that an invasion of England would be unsuccessful. But it could precipitate the one thing he did fear: entry into the war by the United States. Already, in response to Churchill's pleas for intervention, Roosevelt was violating America's neutrality and supplying England with destroyers. The invasion would have to wait, Hitler decided. First, he needed a psychological weapon, one he could use directly on the American people to sap Roosevelt's growing support for war with Germany.

The weapon he needed was in the Vatican. It was no secret that the new Pope, Pius XII, was obsessed with Communism, viewing it as the Anti-Christ threatening to overrun all the Catholic countries of Europe. Hitler would use this obsession to obtain the weapon he needed, a concordat with the Pope that would be published to the world. In the concordat Hitler would agree to abandon any invasion of England, and hurl his formidable forces instead against Communist Russia. When he had defeated the Red army, he would negotiate a peace with France and England, relinquishing all his territorial gains in the west. In exchange for this, the Pope would agree in the concordat that all Hitler's prior actions were justified by the harshness of the Versailles Treaty and that, as a Catholic, he shared the Pope's deep concern about preserving Christianity in Germany and the rest of Europe. It did not matter to Hitler that he never intended to keep his side of the bargain. He knew what affect the publication of such a concordat would have on the Catholics in America, without whose support Roosevelt would not be able to continue his anti-German policy.

Borielli stared into the darkness of the room. The puzzle, however, was still not complete. Missing was the most important piece: the document itself. He wondered what had happened to it.

The Vatican, May 1977 . . .

Cardinal Borielli assessed the situation. It was a mix of bad news and good news. The bad news was that more than six months had passed since Franco's death and what the Spanish Dictator had done with the missing concordat was still a mystery. Monsignor Grappi had been back to Spain a dozen times to interview the Generalissimo's closest friends and all the members of his family, but without success. The good news was that no one Grappi interviewed had ever heard of the document. Its existence was still a secret. Borielli smiled to himself. He had also kept secret the discovery of its signature page. Deeply troubled about the direction the liberal majority in the *Curia* was taking the Church, he planned, when he had the missing portion, to alter that direction. And it was essential to his plan that no one knew of the existence of either portion.

The original Concordat had to exist somewhere, he told himself. Franco would not have destroyed it; he must have hidden it somewhere. But where? Borielli shrugged. Wherever it was, Grappi would eventually find it. No one was more resourceful than his loyal Monsignor, who would leave no stone unturned in his search. In the meantime, he would go forward with his plan.

The Vatican, November 1977 . . .

Borielli put his magnifying glass back down on his desk. He glanced at the tall grandfather clock in the corner of his office. It was almost noon. Downstairs in the great rotunda of Saint Peter's, Pope Paul was just finishing his weekly public Mass, in which he noted in his homily that it was the second anniversary of General Franco's death, asking everyone to remember the Generalissimo, a devout Catholic, in their prayers. Borielli smiled at the irony. While the Pope had been delivering his pro forma tribute, Borielli had been studying the Spanish dictator's posthumous gift; the signatures together of Pius XII and Hitler on a document the contents of which were still unknown to the world.

But it was not the signatures Borielli had been studying. They were genuine, he knew that. What he had been examining closely with his magnifying glass was the ragged edge of the paper where it had been torn from the rest of the document. He nodded his head. Yes, the ragged edge; that was the key. Pope Paul had cancer; everyone in the Vatican knew it. It was only a matter of time before the College of Cardinals would have to assemble to elect his successor. Borielli himself would not be considered; he had too many enemies, among them the powerful leader of the Liberals, Cardinal Vitagliano, who was intent on returning the Church to the ecumenicalism of Pope John XXIII. Vitagliano had already chosen his candidate: Archbishop Luciani of Venice. Borielli's face darkened at the thought of the Venetian. To Borielli, Luciani was more than a liberal; he was a dangerous radical whose elevation to the throne was unthinkable.

Borielli returned to examining the torn piece of paper. He reviewed again in his mind the complex plan he had formulated. While the search for the missing Concordat continued, he would use his unique skill to create an imitation, a perfect forgery full of solemn promises by Hitler that Europe's Jews would not be persecuted by the Nazis. That the German dictator broke his promises would not matter. The substitute document would be hailed by the Vatican as proof that they were extracted from Hitler by Pius XII whose reputation for anti-Semitism still stubbornly hung like a dark cloud over the Vatican. Once the forgery was completed, he would maneuver Vitagliano into accepting it as authentic and announcing the discovery to the world. Then, armed with the real Concordat, he would be in a position to expose Vitagliano as the perpetrator of a monstrous fraud. Borielli rubbed his thin hands together. He would not have to go that far. The threat alone would be enough to ensure that Luciani spent the rest of his life as Archbishop of Venice.

The Vatican, June 1978 . . .

Borielli waited for the ink to dry on the last page of the document he had created. Then, spreading the pages out on his desk, he compared them with the elaborate script of the jurat above the signatures on the torn piece of paper Grappi brought from Madrid. The writing was identical. He smiled; thirty-six years had not diminished his gift. His document must be aged, but that was not a problem. Rome was full of art restorers who supplement their incomes with the reverse process, palming off phony masterpieces on the tourists.

He looked again at the last page of the document. The next step was the critical one; it had to be done with the greatest of care. He decided to rest a few minutes. He stood up and walked to the window. He looked down at the Papal Gardens below. The trees were bare, the grass around them dormant brown. He glanced at the sky. It was dark and threatening. A few drops of rain appeared on the window and trickled erratically down toward the sill. Others joined them and before long it was raining too hard for him to see out. He walked back to his desk and sat down again. He picked up the torn piece of paper and placed it over the space he had left on the last page of his document. He held them tightly together and with sharp scissors cut horizontally across both at the same time, carefully keeping only a few centimeters below the torn piece of paper's ragged edge. He looked at the result. Vitagliano and his experts would wonder why the jurat and signatures were separate from the rest of the document. But in the end, they would have to accept it as authentic because of the unique script common to both. He studied the thin ragged strip he had cut from the torn piece. He smiled. When the real concordat was found, it also would have a ragged edge. The two ragged edges would fit together like two jigsaw puzzle pieces and be irrefutable proof that the document published by Vitagliano was a blatant forgery.

The Hague, July 1, 1978 . . .

It was going to be another hot, humid day in The Hague. The morning commuters streaming off the trains at the central railroad station were already peeling off their jackets and rolling up their shirtsleeves. As Jan Osterbeek stepped down from the 8:15 he felt the sticky wetness under his arms but decided to keep his jacket on. He joined the other commuters making their way along the platform into the terminal. As soon as he was inside the terminal, he stopped at a newspaper kiosk, dropped a half guilder on the wooden counter, and picked up the morning edition of *Het Tag*. He saw on the front page that it was the anniversary of the Israeli's raid on Entebbe, the day they showed the world again that Jews were not just shopkeepers. He tucked the paper under his arm and walked out into the busy Frans Hals Square.

The article about the Entebbe raid triggered memories of his own experiences during World War II. Despite all the years that had passed, what happened in Italy was still vivid in his mind. He reached the far side of the square and started down the *Altmaar Gracht*, the narrow cobblestone street along the main canal leading to the city's business district. His thoughts returned to the present.

In another month he would be twenty-five years with the same company, *Fruitema International BbN*. He could then retire if he wanted. He had thought about it. For the last twelve years, he had held the same routine job, watching a succession of younger men climb past him up the corporate ladder. Now, at sixty-two, he was beyond any hope of promotion. Still, he was not going to retire. The small pension he would receive would barely be enough to live on. Besides, as a widower, childless, and with few friends, his job, although dull and unchallenging, was at least something to do.

He arrived at the building where he worked and went downstairs to the cafeteria for his morning coffee. The cafeteria as usual was crowded and noisy, everyone smoking cigarettes, the air stale and acrid. Today it had the added smell of body odor. He shuffled through the line at the counter to get his coffee, found a table with an empty chair, and sat down. He took out a cigar and lit it, adding more smoke to the room.

Then he settled down to read his paper. The news all seemed just more of what he had read yesterday. He continued reading until he finished his coffee. Then he folded the paper and threw it on the table. As he started to get up, he saw an item on the last page that made him stop. The item caused something in the back of his mind to stir. It was as if he had just remembered an old photograph he had put away somewhere and forgotten. He sat down, picked up the paper again and read the item carefully. It was a wire service report of an article in the Italian newspaper *L'Observatore*.

POPE PIUS XII PROTECTED JEWS FROM HITLER
RECENTLY DISCOVERED DOCUMENT SHOWS

ROME - Pope Pius XII, accused of anti-Semitism during World War II, in fact obtained Hitler's promise not to persecute the Jews, a recently discovered document shows.

The document, found among the papers of the late General Franco of Spain, is a Concordat signed by Pope Pius XII and the German dictator in March 1941 . . .

Osterbeek stopped reading and closed his eyes. He tried to visualize what was in the photograph he had forgotten. It was too old and faded for him to be able to see what it showed. He continued reading.

. . . The Concordat, handwritten in Latin and German, contains Hitler's express promise that all Jews in Germany and in German occupied countries will be treated humanely . . .

He closed his eyes again. The picture in the photograph was beginning to look familiar. He continued reading.

. . . According to a Vatican spokesman, Cardinal Vitagliano, the Concordat was found with the lower portion of the last page separate from the rests of the document. Although the Cardinal offered no explanation for this, he said the document was unquestionably authentic because both parts were written in the same unique script.

He closed his eyes again. He could now see clearly what the photograph showed. It was a picture of a small, dark, vault-like room full of cobwebs. He smiled. The Vatican was lying; only the signature portion of the document could have been found with Franco's papers; the rest of it was not there. The Vatican did not have the real Concordat, and had published a forgery. Osterbeek leaned back in his chair. His whole world had suddenly changed. He knew something the Vatican did not; he knew where the real Concordat was - it was in the picture in the photograph.

Brookline, Massachusetts, July 7, 1978 . . .

Cathy's fingers flew back and forth over the keys in the final crescendo of Chopin's Scherzo in C Sharp Minor. She reached the coda and stretched them to hold the last cord until the sound faded away. She smiled, satisfied with herself. She had played the entire difficult piece without a single mistake. She began playing again, this time the much easier *Clair de Lune* that had been the Judge's favorite. Cathy, still young and attractive, was barely twenty when she married Federal Judge Charles Everett Parkman, a widower with two grown Children. Their May-December marriage raised everyone's eyebrows. No one gave it a chance; it was just an ephemeral product of the Judge's climacteric and his young law clerk's infatuation with him, everyone thought. But they were wrong; the marriage lasted, the age difference between Cathy and the

Judge proved important only to everyone else. The ten years they spent together, before the Judge's stroke, were the happiest for both of them. The stroke was a massive one that left the Judge completely paralyzed, his mind cruelly imprisoned in his own body, his once extraordinary vocabulary reduced to meaningless animal sounds. His death almost a year later had been considered a blessing.

Cathy found herself thinking about the Judge as she played the Debussy classic. Oh, how he loved to hear her play it, she remembered; she must have played it for him hundreds of times. She smiled to herself, remembering the time she teased him, saying she would not play it for him anymore until he taught her the sonata that he was always so mysterious about. The strange sonata; she had not thought about it for years. She began playing it and then heard the front door open. She called over her shoulder. "Who is it?"

"It's me." The voice belonged to Joe Biancalana who followed his answer into the room. Biancalana, who was two years younger than Cathy, tall and muscular with a ruggedly handsome face, gave her a big kiss and sat down beside her on the piano bench. "I called the Club. We've got the grass courts at two-thirty if you still want to play. But I have to tell you: it's awfully hot out."

Cathy shrugged. "I'd still like to play."

"You sure?"

"I'm sure; I don't mind the heat."

Biancalana had entered Cathy's life two years earlier. Both were members of the Longwood Tennis Club and found themselves paired as partners in a blind draw tournament. They played well together and liked each other. More because of the latter than the former, they agreed over gin and tonics on the clubhouse veranda to enter as a team in the Annual

Labor Day Tournament. They went on to win the tournament and to like each other even more. That was the beginning . . .

Biancalana gave Cathy a gentle poke on the shoulder. "Okay, we'll play but don't expect me to go easy on you just because it's hot. I'm going to run your pretty fanny all over the court to make up for the last time we played."

Cathy smiled. "You mean when I won both sets?"

Biancalana made a face and looked out toward the kitchen.

"What have you got to drink out there that's cold?"

Cathy was still smiling. "Both sets, remember?"

Biancalana laughed. "Okay, okay, both sets: I was off my game that day. Now, what have you got that's cold?"

Cathy pointed to a pitcher of iced tea on the piano. "You can have some of that but you'll have to get a glass. Or, there's beer in the fridge."

Biancalana got up. "I think I'll have the beer. You want anything?"

Cathy shook her head. "No thanks, I've already had two glasses of iced tea." She began playing again. When Biancalana came back from the kitchen, she saw that he was frowning. "What's the matter, Joe?"

He pointed to the piano. "What the hell is that you're playing? I've never heard you play anything like that before."

Cathy stopped playing. "It's nothing, really, it's just -" She reached for the pitcher on the piano. "I've changed my mind. I think I'll have some more iced tea after all."

Biancalana laughed and sat down beside her again. "I didn't mean for you to stop. It's just that I never heard you play anything like that before. It sounded like background music for a vampire movie. What the hell was it?"

"Oh, just something Charles taught me a long time ago."

"The Judge taught it to you?" Biancalana was surprised. "I thought you told me he couldn't play a note."

"He couldn't except for this."

Biancalana frowned. "Sounded pretty complicated for someone who couldn't play at all."

"He memorized it."

Biancalana was even more surprised. "Memorized it?"

Cathy nodded. "He said he just played it over and over and over until he had memorized it."

"Wow! I'm impressed! But why the hell did he do that?"

"He would never tell me."

"So you must have asked him why?"

"Yes."

"What did he say?"

"He said it was something he had to do when he was in the war, something he couldn't tell me about. All I could ever get out of him was that it was part of an old sonata some Italian monk had written."

Biancalana took a sip of his beer. "Wasn't the Judge in the OSS during the war?"

"I'm not sure it was the OSS. I know that he was in Italy, though, because I remember he told me once about parachuting behind the enemy lines there. Something went wrong and he was captured. That's all I know; he would never tell me anything more."

"How come he taught you that thing you were playing?"

Cathy smiled. "Because I pestered him so much about it. For a long time he refused to teach it to me. He said it was better I didn't know how to play it. But you know me, Joe, the more someone tells me I shouldn't do something, the more I want to do it. I just kept pestering him, and he finally gave in. But he made me promise never to let anyone know I could play it."

Biancalana laughed. "Well, now I know."

Cathy nodded. "Yes." She turned and looked at him. "But you are not the only one, Joe."

"Oh? Who else has heard you play it?"

"No one."

Bianalana frowned. "No one? Then how -?"

She shook her head. "I don't know."

Biancalana was confused. "Wait a minute, I'm lost. If no one else has heard you play it, how can -?"

Cathy stood up and walked across the room to her telephone table. She picked up a note she had written, brought it back and handed it to Biancalana. On it was written: "Jan Osterbeek, 011 31 30 734268." Biancalana looked up at her. "What's this?"

"It's the telephone number of someone in *The Hague.*"

"You mean *The Hague* in Holland?"

"Yes."

"Who is she?"

Cathy smiled. "It's a he. I don't know who he is; he just said he –"

"You mean you've talked to the guy?"

Cathy sat down beside him. "He telephoned me a few days ago. He said he was an old friend of Charles; he said they were in the war together. He didn't know Charles had died. He said he was calling because something had happened recently that made it imperative he have the notes to the sonata Charles learned in Italy. He was distressed to hear that Charles had died. He said they went through a lot together during the war, that Charles had saved his life in Italy." She paused. "Then he said something odd."

"What?"

"He said 'Thank God you can play the sonata.'"

Biancalana frowned. "How did he know that?"

Cathy shook her head. "I don't know. I pretended at first I didn't know what he was talking about. But I could tell he didn't believe me. He said the notes to the sonata were of an unbelievable value and that with them he can obtain an enormous sum of money which, as Charles's widow, I will be entitled to share. He said he was coming over to explain everything to me."

Biancalana finished his beer. "Did he say why the notes to the sonata were so valuable?"

Cathy shook her head. "No, he didn't say."

Biancalana laughed derisively. "I'll bet he didn't say anything either about how much money you are going to get."

Cathy looked at him. "Yes, he did, Joe."

Biancalana waited. "Well?"

Cathy turned to him and put her hands in his. "Joe, he said my share will be a half a million dollars!

Over the Italian Coast, January 21, 1944 . . .

Parkman's earphones crackled. It was the pilot. "Are you there, Major?"

"I'm here."

"We're just passing over the Italian coast now; I thought you'd like to know."

"I suppose that means the end of the pleasure part of this trip."

"I'm afraid so, Major, we're over enemy territory now and have to expect some flak being thrown up at us. You may want to warn the others that it's likely to get a little bumpy."

Parkman turned to the 'three men cramped with him in the bomb bay of the B-24 Liberator. Like him, they were all wearing khaki-black jumpsuits and heavy turtle-neck sweaters, their faces blackened with charcoal, Sten guns slung across their chests between their parachute straps. He told them what the pilot had said.

Lancaster, the only one who had jumped before, smiled. "Let's hope all we have to worry about is flak. If we run into fighters, they'll shoot us down like a clay pigeon." He nudged the man beside him. "A *pigeon d'argile*, eh Mollet?"

Mollet's response was a stream of French punctuated with expletives. Lancaster laughed and turned to the third man. "You understand French, Jan, what the hell was that all about?"

The Dutchman shrugged. "He's just complaining again that this whole mission is crazy."

"What do you think, Jan?"

"I don't know. Maybe, if we're lucky . . ."

Parkman was only half listening to their conversation. His mind was back in Benghazi where they had all been briefed on "Operation Bisect," the operation the Allies hoped would shorten the war in Italy by months and save thousands of lives. The operation seemed straight forward enough. The German Twelfth Army under General Kesselring was four hundred miles south of Rome, dug in along the Gustav Line to stop Patton and Montgomery who were pouring troops into Italy from Sicily. In less than twenty-four hours, the American VI

Corps, under General Lucas, would make a surprise landing high up the Italian coast at the small resort town of Anzio. Lucas would establish a beachhead, then break out and drive east all the way to the Adriatic, sealing Kesselring off in the shoe of the Italian boot. Hitler would learn of the landing , figure out what the Allies were up to, and rush his panzers down from France to extricate Kesselring. Parkman smiled. That is where the Italian partisans would come in. Simultaneously with Lucas's breakout, a wave of sabotage would hit all the major rail and communication centers in northern Italy, vital to Hitler's movement of his panzers south. Lucas would have time to strengthen his line and when the panzers did arrive it would be too late. Kesselring, his supplies and reinforcements cut off by the VI Corps, and pressure from Patton and Montgomery increasing daily, would be squeezed into surrendering.

The whole operation hinged on two things: one, Lucas would have to break out from Anzio quickly before Kesselring smelled a rat and moved his Twelfth Army north to Rome; two, the partisans would have to do their job. The latter was the reason the lone Liberator containing Parkman and the others was now winging its way through the moonless sky over the remote Italian countryside. In half an hour, it would be above the drop zone; its bomb bay doors would open and Parkman and his group would jump out into the cold dark night. The partisans would be waiting on the ground to take them up into the mountains where they could coordinate the efforts of the partisans with the breakout at Anzio.

Parkman had read the dossiers of the three men assigned to the mission with him. Lancaster was a British commando who had already killed more than his share of Germans in night raids on the occupied French coast. Mollet, a *Poilu,* had been among the Frenchmen evacuated at Dunkirk because he was one of their best demolition men. Osterbeek was recruited from the Dutch underground. Fluent in a dozen languages, including Italian and German, he knew better than anyone else what made the Krauts tick.

Parkman had read his own dossier as well. In it he saw he was commended for coolness at the battle of the Kasserine Pass where the Americans fought the Germans for the first time since World War I and did not do well. Kasserine may have been the reason he was chosen to lead this mission but he doubted it. The reason was more likely political, not military. Eisenhower wanted the mission led by an American but not one who would put a lot of English noses out of joint. The way Parkman figured it, he was picked for no better reason than that he had been a Rhodes Scholar and it could be said he lived in England at least for a time.

The pilot's voice crackled in the earphones again. "We're picking up ground lights, Major; we can expect flak anytime now."

Parkman spoke into the little graphite transmitter on his chest. "What about fighters?"

"Not likely. Remember, we're dealing with the Italians, not the Germans. They don't like to fight unless they have to. And we're a single plane without any escort. My guess is they'll think we're either crippled or off course, not worth sending fighters up for."

"I hope you're right. Thanks." Parkman took off his headset and told the others what the pilot had said.

Mollet was still complaining. *"Merde!* This whole thing is crazy! The partisans cannot stop the Panzers. I have seen what the Panzers can do; they will just -"

Lancaster cut him off. "Look, Pierre, we've all fought Jerry and know how tough he is. Jan, here, probably knows better than any of us. Maybe you're right, that this whole mission is a bit of madness. But there's not really anything we can do now except give it a go, is there? "

Mollet started to say something when, suddenly, the plane was rocked by an explosion. It was followed by another, and then another. Parkman's headset came alive with the pilot's voice talking to his crew. "We're into it now, men; they've spotted us and are sending up their welcoming bouquets." The voice paused. "You on, Major?"

"I'm on."

"They're throwing up more flak than I expected. And we're still twenty minutes from your drop zone. Tell your men to hang on; I'm going to take us up another thousand feet to see if I can-" His voice was cut off by another explosion, this one so close it made the whole plane shudder. The pilot called to one of his turret gunners. "Turner!"

"Yeah, Skipper?"

"We just took a hit, one of the port engines. It's on fire; I can see the flames."

"I can see them too, now."

"Turner, listen up."

"I'm listening, Skipper."

"Keep your eye on that engine. It's still giving me some prop, so I'm going to keep the ignition on until I can get more altitude. I'll need all four engines to get this crate up out of this stuff. But I don't like those flames, so keep an eye on them. If they start spreading inboard, give a yell. I don't want them anywhere near the main fuel tank."

"Gotcha, Skipper; I'll watch 'em like a hawk."

The whole sky was now erupting with flak, the lethal clouds full of pieces of jagged steel that could tear the wings and fuselage of the Liberator to shreds. Another explosion rocked the plane. It was on Turner's side and the pilot got on the intercom to him again. "Turner?"

This time there was no response.

"Turner?"

Still no response.

"Come on, Turner, answer!"

The pilot switched to the other turret gunner. "Evans, what's the story back there? What's the matter with Turner?"

"I don't know, Skipper. I'm trying to get myself turned around so I can see. Everything's all smashed up here and there's a lot of smoke. I can't see a thing! I'm trying to get over to Turner's side now." There was a pause, "Holy Shit!"

"What's the matter, Evans?"

"Jesus Christ! The whole side of the ship where Turner was is gone! Nothing's there but a big hole! I can see the whole sky out through it!"

The pilot's voice remained calm. "Okay, okay, get back on your own side, and strap yourself in. Stay the hell away from that hole; I don't want you getting sucked out through it too."

The plane was jolted by another explosion and pitched violently from one side to the other throwing Parkman and the others forward so their restraining straps cut into their shoulders, then back hard against the fuselage. Parkman heard the pilot calling to the tail gunner. "Dombrowski!"

"Yeah, Skipper?" "You okay back there?" "I'm okay. But that last one hit us right in the ass. It blew off half the tail section."

Parkman had heard enough. He turned to the others. "It's no good, men; we're not going to make it. The pilot's telling everyone to bail out. He's going to open the bomb bay doors for us. When he opens them, Lancaster, you go first. Then you, Mollet, and then you Jan. And remember, all of you, when you hit the ground, get rid of your chute right away. Bury it, then look for the rest of us."

The whole plane was now shaking violently and Parkman and the others had to grab the struts of the fuselage to keep from being tossed down into the bomb bay. Their eyes were fixed on the steel doors, waiting for them to open. They opened and a blast of frigid air rushed up into their blackened faces. Through the opening they could see the cold, black night outside and hear the straining whine of the plane's engines as it spiraled downward out of control.

Lancaster released his grip on the fuselage and slid down to the opening. He looked back at the others, gave the thumbs-up sign, and then dropped through the opening out of sight. Mollet went next, still shaking his head and swearing as he disappeared into the cold darkness. It was now Osterbeek's turn. The Dutchman slid down and threw his legs into the opening. He looked back at Parkman. "See you on the ground, Major." He crossed himself and jumped. Parkman watched the Dutchman disappear like the others. Then he let go of the fuselage, tore off his headset, and slid down to the bottom of the bomb bay. He was trying to get his legs into the opening when heard a deep rumbling sound. It was coming from inside the plane and getting louder and louder, like the sound of a locomotive rushing towards him. He struggled to get his legs into the opening but the bomber, still shaking violently, rolled upside down, throwing him back against the fuselage. The rumbling, louder than ever, was reaching a crescendo.

It's too late, he thought, the whole plane is going to blow up! He closed his eyes and stiffened his body as the sound of the locomotive thundered into the bomb bay and enveloped him.

Suddenly, everything was strangely quiet. Parkman, his eyes, still closed, listened. There was no sound at all. The rumbling was gone. He could not even hear the whining of the engines any more. He opened his eyes and then quickly closed them again. No! - that can't be right!, he told himself. He opened his eyes again slowly. He still could not believe what he was seeing. The plane was not there; the entire B-24 Liberator bomber had disappeared and he was standing in the middle of nowhere. He looked all around. There was nothing but a gray emptiness stretching away from him in every direction as far as he could see. He listened. There was no sound at all, only an eerie silence. He shook his head, puzzled. Where the hell was the plane? What the hell had happened to it? He remembered the loud rumbling sound and thinking it was going to blow up, but it didn't - or did it? No, he would have been blown up with it, Wait a minute, maybe - no, that couldn't be. But what if it is? That would explain why he didn't remember. But then that would mean that . . . He made a wry smile. Okay, so that's what must have happened. It's the only explanation. The plane blew up before he could get out and he was killed. He managed a nervous laugh. Well, I guess that's it, he thought. I've finally bought it, and I'm now in some in-between place where they make you wait while they decide what to do with you. He stood there wondering what was going to happen next.

He heard something! The sound was a rat-a-tat coming out of the nothingness below him. He listened for a moment and then his face widened. He recognized the sound. It was the Liberator's turret guns firing. He realized what was happening.

Holy Jesus! I'm falling! He fumbled for the ripcord on his parachute and pulled it as hard as he could. The canvas pack on his chest exploded open and three hundred feet of black silk rushed up past his face. It snapped into a huge umbrella over his head, yanking him up like a puppet on a string. For several minutes, he swung widely back and forth. Then, gradually, he settled into a steady vertical descent. A gust of wind caught him just as he hit the ground. He lost his balance and tumbled into a row of dormant grapevines. He scrambled to his feet, ran to where his parachute had fallen, and threw himself on top of it. He took a minute to catch his breath, and then stood up, gathered the parachute into a ball and put his foot on it. He took off his harness and looked around. The night was moonless and he could barely see anything in the darkness. He knew he had landed in a vineyard, but that was all. He listened. The only sound was the rustling of the wind through the rows of empty vines. He reached in his pocket and took out a small object. He smiled. Some things never change, he thought, the little clicker in his hand was no different than the one he had as a kid. He slipped it between his thumb and forefinger and squeezed. Even the sharp metallic sound was the same. After three clicks, he stopped and listened. He heard an answering click. He signaled again and waited. This time the answer was closer. He signaled once more and then began digging a hole to bury his parachute.

Lancaster was the first to appear out of the darkness, his blackened face and accentuated white eyes reminding Parkman of a minstrel man. They exchanged glances and then stood still to listen for the others.

A few minutes later, Mollet and Osterbeek who had landed close together, joined them. Mollet had twisted his ankle and was leaning on the Dutchman for support. Parkman motioned for Lancaster to give Osterbeek a hand, then spoke to all of them. "It looks like we've been lucky. I kept my eye out on the way down and didn't see anything that looks like a town around here. I think we've landed away from where there might be troops stationed."

Lancaster pointed in the direction he had come. "I saw a small light over that way. It looked like it could be coming from a farmhouse."

Parkman thought for a minute, "Okay, let's head in that direction and find out what it is." He told Lancaster to lead the way and took Lancaster's place helping Osterbeek with the injured Frenchman.

The four of them made their way slowly through the darkness, stopping each time they thought they heard something. But it was always just the wind. The vineyard seemed to go on forever. Finally they came to the end of it. The rows of vines stopped at a dirt road. Beyond it was the light Lancaster had seen. Parkman motioned for the others to stay where they were and crossed the road alone. He crept slowly toward the light. As he drew closer, he could see that it was coming from a window in a huge stone building that loomed out of the darkness. He crept closer and then stopped. He saw that the light was coming from a stained glass window.

Valdarno, Italy, January 26, 1944 . . .

They had been hiding in the wine cellar of the abbey for five days; it was time to leave, Parkman decided. Mollet's ankle had healed enough to walk on, and staying any longer would endanger the lives of the monks who were giving them sanctuary.

It was the middle of the night. Parkman was the only one still awake. He could hear the others snoring under the heavy blankets the monks had provided. The wine cellar was damp and cold. He rubbed his hands together to keep them warm as he hunched over the small wooden table studying the map he had spread out under the light of a candle. It was the twenty-sixth, four days since the Allied landing at Anzio. By now, he estimated, the American VI Corps must be a hundred kilometers in from the coast. There was no point thinking about the mission anymore, he told himself; the only thing to do now was to take his group and head back towards General Lucas's advancing army. He folded up the map and stuffed it in his jacket. He picked up the candle and walked back to where the others were sleeping. He wrapped himself in one of the heavy blankets, settled down on the dirt floor beside them, and then blew out the light. As he lay in the darkness waiting to fall asleep, he thought about the strange order of monks who were hiding them. All old men, they were bound by some code of silence that prohibited them from uttering a single word. The only exception was the Abbot, Brother Diego, who had spoken to Parkman briefly in Spanish the night he and the others stumbled in from the vineyard. Osterbeek had translated what he said. He told them that his abbey was the last remnant of a monastic order that had fled from Spain in the sixteenth century. He said Parkman and his group were fortunate to have landed where they did because it was a *"Zone tranquillo,"* a quiet part of the country where there were few soldiers. Only rarely, he said, did the Germans ever - Parkman's thoughts were interrupted by a sound at the door to the wine cellar. He looked up and saw one of the monks standing in the doorway, framed in the light from the monks' dormitory above the wine cellar. He got up and went to see what he wanted. The monk handed him a note that was written in Spanish. Parkman took it back to where Osterbeek was sleeping. He woke up the Dutchman and showed him the note.

"What does it say?"

"It's from the Abbot. He wants to see you."

"Now?"

"Yes, right away. He's waiting for you in his study."

"Okay. You'd better come too."

Osterbeek threw off his blanket and stood up. Parkman motioned for the monk to show them the way. The monk waited for them to come up the stone steps to where he was standing, and then took them into the abbey where they found themselves in the chapel. The monk led them across the transept, past a large ornate organ, and into the sacristy. He pointed to one of the doors in the sacristy, and then turned and left. Parkman tapped on the door and then opened it. Inside, Brother Diego was standing, warming his hands at a fireplace. His face was clouded with concern. He began speaking to them excitedly in Spanish. Osterbeek translated what he was saying. ". . . He says he has distressing news, that the situation outside has deteriorated dramatically, that there are reports of German troops in great numbers moving up from the south. He says a large force of Americans landed on the coast west of here several days ago and that - "

Osterbeek stopped, his face widening in surprise at what the Abbot was saying. He turned to Parkman. "He says they're still there at Anzio!" Parkman was incredulous. "At Anzio! You mean they haven't advanced at all?"

"That's what he says. I don't understand it either. For some reason, Lucas is keeping the whole VI Corps inside the perimeter of the beachhead." Osterbeek listened again to the Abbot.

" . . . He says the Germans are puzzled too, but they are not wasting any time. Kesselring is moving his entire army north as fast as he can."

Parkman frowned. "That means in a few days this whole place will be crawling with Krauts." He thought for a moment. "Tell him we appreciate everything he's done for us, that we're getting out of here right now."

Osterbeek told the Abbot what Parkman had said. The Abbot shook his head. ". . . He says it's too late for us to get away, that we'd be captured whatever direction we went, and that the Germans would then trace us back to the abbey. He says the wine cellar is no longer safe and that he is going to have to hide us in another place. That's why he summoned you here tonight, to tell you that. And he says there is something else he must explain to you."

"Tell him I'm listening."

The Abbot motioned for them to sit down on the wooden bench in front of the fireplace and then began speaking again. ". . . He says the monks here are all old men, that even the youngest, Brother Lupo, is well past the biblical age. He says they're the last of a religious order discredited by the Church many years ago, only tolerated now by Rome because time will soon complete their extinction anyway. He says at one time their order flourished throughout all Spain and something he keeps referring to as their 'treasure' was accepted by the Church as a glorification of God. But then, he says, their enemies rose up in the councils of the Holy See, condemned the treasure as grotesque and pagan, and sent teams of priests out from Madrid to destroy it."

Parkman interrupted. "Does he say what this 'treasure' is?"

". . . He says that only one monastery of the monks of his order were able to escape to Italy with the treasure." Osterbeek paused and looked at Parkman. "Why the hell do you suppose he's telling us all this anyway?"

Parkman shook his head. "I don't know. Let him go on."

The Abbot continued.

". . . He says that behind the stone steps leading down to the wine cellar from the monks' dormitory there is a door concealed as part of the wall. It is the door to a secret room where their treasure is hidden. He says it is in that room we will have to hide if the Germans come."

The Abbot paused to poke the coals in the fireplace. Then he began speaking again, now looking directly at Parkman. ". . . He says what he is going to tell you will break a sacred vow of secrecy he has taken but he is breaking the vow because it is the only way to save us from the Germans. He says the door to the secret room can be opened only when notes of a certain sonata are played on the organ in the chapel. He says a mechanism buried beneath the abbey connects the bellows of the organ to a lock at the bottom of the door, and the tumblers of the lock are tripped by the sequence of notes played. He says the sonata is an unwritten one that has been passed down from abbot to abbot for centuries so only the monks of the order can play it and open the door.

Osterbeek paused and looked at Parkman, still puzzled why the Abbot was telling them all of this. Parkman, his eyes now fixed on the Abbot's, motion for the Dutchman to continue. " . . . He says he is concerned that the Germans may come suddenly, without warning, while he and the others are out in the vineyard, too far from the chapel to get back in time to open the door. He is going to teach you the notes of the sonata so you can unlock it. He says the task is not a simple one and that you must begin learning it now, tonight."

Parkman managed a smile. "Tell him I don't know one musical note from another, but if he thinks he can teach me, I'm game to give it a shot." The Abbot said something else and Osterbeek frowned. Parkman looked at the Dutchman. "What did he just say?""He said I should return to the wine cellar, that the secret should be shared only with you."

"Anything else?"

"The rest was just muttering."

"What was he muttering?" "Just asking God to forgive him, that's all."

Parkman stood up. He put his hand on the Abbot's shoulder and looked into his eyes. "Tell him I understand what it means to him to have to break his vow. And tell him this. Tell him he has my sacred vow that his secret will always be safe with me."

Valdarno, Italy, February 2, 1944 . . .

Osterbeek held his wristwatch up close to the flickering candle. It was almost midnight. Parkman had been gone an hour. He looked across the wooden table in the wine cellar at Lancaster and Mollet. A week had passed since he had shared with them the Abbot's story about the secret room. They had all agreed to wait until tonight to make their move. He took a crumpled piece of paper from his pocket and flattened it out on the table. "I've made a note each time the Major has gone to learn to play the sonata, showing what time he left and what time he returned." He ran his finger down the column of figures on the piece of paper. "You can see that he stays at least two hours, sometimes longer, but never less than that. And we know from what he told me, that the sessions always begin with the Abbot playing the notes for him first."

Lancaster leaned forward over the table. "This must unlock the door?"

"Yes. And it remains that way until the session is over and the Abbot comes down to lock it again." Mollet became impatient. "Why the hell are we just sitting here talking? I say we go now and find out what the treasure is that they've got hidden there."

Lancaster nodded. "I agree." Osterbeek put the paper with his notes on it back in his jacket and stood up. He picked up the candle. "All right, let's do it." Carrying the flickering candle in front of him, he led the way back to the foot of the stone steps leading up to the monk's dormitory. They all stopped there and listened. They could faintly hear the organ being played.

Osterbeek reached with the candle into the dark recess behind the steps. In the flickering light, they saw the stone door, made to appear as part of the wall, now ajar. Osterbeek pulled the door open more, and the three of them squeezed past it into the pitch darkness beyond it. When they were all inside, Osterbeek held the candle up over his head. They all gasped. They were in a narrow vault-like room covered with cobwebs. Along the walls on both sides hideous skeletons of old monks were standing in shallow alcoves, their bony faces grinning out from under dusty monastic hoods. Above, the entire ceiling was decorated with human bones from every part of the body, arranged in bizarre patterns.

Lancaster's bulldog face widened. "It's a bloody crypt!" Mollet turned angrily to Osterbeek. "There's no treasure in here."

The Dutchman was not listening to either of them. Something at the back of the room had caught his attention, and he had dropped down on one knee to examine it. It was a small iron chest. Like everything else in the room, it was covered with cobwebs. He brushed away the ones on the lid of the chest and tried to open it. It was locked. Lancaster knelt down beside him to pry it open with his commando knife.

Mollet had not joined them. He was still standing by the first skeleton, staring at it. The more he looked at it, the more it seemed to be laughing at him. Frustrated, he swore at it and smashed his fist into its bony face. It collapsed like a house of cards into a pile of splintered bones on the floor at his feet. Lancaster was making progress with the lock on the lid of the chest. It was loosening. He slipped his knife in further and twisted it with both hands. The lock snapped. He lifted the lid and looked inside the chest. "It's empty; there's nothing here but some papers tied with a yellow ribbon."

Osterbeek took the papers out and looked at them.

"What are they, Jan?" "I don't know. They're all written in German and Latin. They look like pages of an agreement of some sort."

"Agreement between whom?"

"I can't tell. The bottom of the last page, where the signatures would be, has been torn off and isn't here." He continued to study the papers. "They're full of stuff about Communists and Jews and -"

There was a noise outside the door. Someone was coming down the stone steps into the wine cellar. They all turned toward the door. The Abbot appeared, his wrinkled face twisted in astonishment. He threw up his arms in protest and rushed into the room. He did not see the bones of the fallen skeleton, tripped over them, and fell forward on the floor. He uttered a sharp cry of pain, rolled over on his back and lay motionless. One of the splintered bones was sticking out of his chest. Mollet looked down at him and then at Osterbeek and Lancaster. "Jesus Christ! He's dead! Let's get the hell out of here!"

Osterbeek re-tied the papers and threw them back in the chest. The three of them ran out of the room. They pushed the stone door closed and started back to the other end of the wine cellar. They stopped. Two German soldiers were coming down the stone steps with *Schmeissers* pointed at them. Osterbeek put his hands up over his head. Lancaster and Mollet did the same.

The Germans marched them outside. There were gray uniforms everywhere, swarming over the abbey, rounding up the monks and lining them up against one of the walls. Parkman had been captured and was being shoved towards one of the half-tracks. He saw Osterbeek and the others and called to them. "Where's Brother Diego, have you seen him?"

Osterbeek glanced at Lancaster and Mollet, and then shouted back.

"No, Major, we haven't seen him at all."

The Hague, July 30, 1978 . . .

Osterbeek finished his supper of leftover stew, put the dishes in the sink to be washed later, and went into his small living room. He poured himself a glass of *jenever*, lit up a cigar and settled into his favorite chair. It was now only a matter of time, he told himself. Fate had dealt him a winning hand in a game of enormous stakes. He had only to play the hand right and they would be his. He closed his eyes and reviewed, step by step, what he had accomplished so far.

The first step had been obvious; he had to make certain the document was still there. He took a leave of absence and flew to Florence. There he rented a car and drove to the abbey. The abbey was no longer used as such and was rarely visited by anyone. It was, however, still maintained by the Church and looked after by an old caretaker priest who lived a kilometer away. The old priest gave him a tour of the place. The Germans had blown up the building where the monks slept, burying most of the wine cellar under a pile of rubble. It had never been rebuilt, just left that way with a cross on top of it as a memorial to the monks killed that night. This meant the document was still there, buried under part of the rubble. He had the priest take him inside the abbey to the chapel. He did not need to ask the priest the question he had. The old man showed him the organ and pointed out with obvious pride that, although it was more than a hundred years old, it was still in remarkable working order. He thanked the priest for the tour and left. That took care of step one. The next was not so easy. He took the train to Rome and rented a small flat on the *Via Espagna*, not far from the famous Spanish Steps. He spent the next several weeks visiting the Vatican, pretending to be a writer doing research for an historical novel. He was surprised how the pretense opened doors and mouths for him. Many of the priests he talked to were quite garrulous. It was not long before he was able to piece together some of the puzzle. The document in the crypt was an agreement entered into by Pope Pius XII and Hitler in 1941. After they entered into it, they decided for some reason to give it to Franco, probably to hold until the happening of some event before it could be published, Whatever the event was, it must never have occurred. The fact that Franco did not die until many years later explained why the document's existence had only recently come to light. Parts of the puzzle still remained a mystery. Why did Franco tear off and keep only the signatures? And how did the rest of the document end up in the abbey in *Valdarno?* These were some of the unanswered questions. But they were not the important ones. The important ones were: "Why a forgery? And who in the Vatican was responsible for it?" These were the questions to which he needed the answers if his plan was to succeed.

He suspected at first that the author of the forgery was a Cardinal named Vitagliano, the one who had announced the discovery among Franco's papers. But the more he learned about Vitagliano the more doubtful he became. Vitagliano was the leader of the *Curia's* liberals and the most powerful man in the Vatican second only to the Pope. He had no apparent reason for publishing a forgery, and all indications were he believed the published document to be authentic. No, he decided, Vitagliano was not his man; he had to look for another candidate. He continued his search.He was about to give up when his attention was drawn to a Cardinal Borielli. Borielli, an arch conservative and bitter enemy of Vitagliano, stood to gain politically if the real Concordat could be produced and the leader of the liberal shown to be involved in a fraud. He dug into Borielli's past. He learned that Borielli was a young Vatican priest in 1941 and that only a short time after the date of the Concordat he was made a Monsignor, an elevation highly unusual in light of his youth and inexperience. He dug even deeper and learned that the elevation had been ordered by Pope Pius XII without any consultation at all with *Curia,* again something highly unusual. He knew then that he had his man, that Borielli was somehow involved with the original document and would know the published one was a forgery. He arranged for a meeting with a member of Borielli's staff, a Monsignor Grappi. He told Grappi he had certain information he thought would be of interest to his Cardinal, information that showed beyond any doubt that the document discovered amongst Franco's papers was a forgery. Grappi was polite but patronizing. He said the Cardinal was too busy to see him but he would pass along to His Eminence whatever information Osterbeek had. He told Grappi the information was for the Cardinal's ears only. When the Monsignor said that was impossible, he stood firm, refusing to speak to anyone but the Cardinal. The meeting ended and he left, confident he had made his point, that even if Borielli had nothing to do with the original concordat, he would want to know more about an allegation that the document his arch enemy had published to the world was a forgery. He was right. The next day, he received a telephone call from Grappi telling him the Cardinal would see him. He went back to the Vatican and met with Borielli alone in his office. He put it to the Cardinal in one sentence. He told him he knew the Concordat the Vatican had published was a forgery because he had seen the real Concordat and knew where it was. Osterbeek smiled to himself, remembering Borielli's reaction. The old Cardinal was as cool as a cucumber, saying that was impossible, that the document found amongst Franco's papers had been verified as authentic by experts. He said he had granted the interview only because of the seriousness of the allegation, that he was very busy and had to bring the interview to an end. Osterbeek refilled his glass. The next part of his reverie was worth another *jenever*, he told himself. He stood up and shook hands with the Cardinal. Then, as he was leaving he began describing the document he had seen in the iron chest, quoting verbatim some of the text he remembered. That did it; the look on Borielli's face confirmed his suspicion that the Cardinal was somehow involved in the real concordat. He let Borielli continue his pretense of disbelief, thanked him for the interview, and left. He was certain he would hear from the Cardinal again. He walked back out to the kitchen. Yes, he decided, he had done well so far. But now, still remaining was the third and most difficult step: dealing with the Major's widow.

The Vatican, August 2, 1978 . . .

Borielli scowled as he paced back and forth in his office, his hands clasped behind his back, his long pointed chin buried in his cassock. He was anything but pleased. Events were overtaking his plan. Pope Paul's cancer had spread and was now in an advanced stage. The doctors were talking about less than a month. And Borielli knew he was not the only one with a plan. There were rumors that Vitagliano had met secretly with Luciani and that the Venetian was already making preparations for his ascension.

He continued to pace back and forth, his scowl deepening with each step. It might be too late now to keep Luciani from the throne even if Grappi found the missing Concordat. And the Monsignor, although searching for it night and day, was no closer to finding it than when started three years ago.

Borielli stopped at the window and stared out at St. Peter's Square, now virtually deserted but for a few late afternoon tourists. His hand tightened behind his back. He had no choice now but to deal with the Dutchman. The price he was asking for the document was outrageous. It would mean falsifying the

Vatican accounts, something he would never have dreamed of doing. But now, it was his only course. The direction in which Vitagliano and his liberals were taking the Church could only lead to disaster. No price was too high to prevent this. He had made his decision. His forgery had passed scrutiny by the experts Vitagliano had consulted, and the leader of the liberals had wasted no time in publishing it to the world. The trap had been set, ready to be sprung when the Dutchman delivered to him the missing Concordat. Dealing with the Dutchman would take time, and Luciani might become Pope in the meantime. His face hardened. But that could be taken care of afterwards.

Avignon, France, August 15, 1978 . . .

For a brief period in the 14th Century, the Holy Roman Catholic Church was ruled not from Rome but from the small medieval town of Avignon nestled on the gentle banks of the Rhone in Provence, France.

Today, six centuries later, Avignon is still dominated by the huge fortress-like *Palais de Papes*. Long empty and abandoned, much of it now in ruins, it remains an impressive monument to the futile attempt by a succession of non-Italian Popes to plant the seat of the Holy See permanently in French soil. Every year, thousands of tourists travel to Avignon to see the old *Palais*, walk around its endless rooms and listen to guides describe its brief but colorful history. The tourists for the most part are French. Those who are not pay a few francs for a special guide who is multilingual. It was Sunday afternoon and Pierre Mollet was playing *Belot* with his seventeen year old son, Jean Louis, at the kitchen table. Pierre was winning. He took the final trick and laughed. *"Voila!* That is game!" He gave his son a friendly poke on the shoulder. *"Eh bien, Mon Cher,* I guess it was just my turn to have the luck tonight." Jean Louis pushed his chair back from the table. "I am tired of playing." He looked at his watch. "Mama is late; it is almost six o'clock. I promised my friends I would meet them at the cinema." Pierre gathered up the cards, tapped them into a neat pack, and placed them on the shelf behind him. "She is not late, Jean Louis; Sunday is always her busiest day at the *Palais,* you know that." He smiled. "Yes, when your mother comes home today, her pocketbook will be heavy with francs from the tourists"

His son was clearly out of sorts. "Yes, and with a lot of foreign coins that are worthless."

Pierre laughed. "There will be lots of foreign coins, that is true; but they will not be worthless. I will take them all to the bank tomorrow and exchange them for francs as I always do."

Jean Louis continued to grumble. "I don't understand why Mama has to work anyway. None of my friends' mothers do."

Pierre tried to placate him. "She does not have to work, Jean Louis; she does it because she enjoys being a special guard at the *Palais.* Besides, what else would she do with her time?" Jean Louis stood up. "But none of my friends' mothers work; their fathers all - " He was interrupted by the sound of someone coming in the door from the street below.

Pierre's face brightened. "Ah, that is your mother now. Watch and see if her pocketbook is not fat with coins." Footsteps came quickly up the stairs and a moment later Madam Mollet entered the room. Short and shaped like the brush of a broom, she had a round pleasant face that broke into a smile when she saw her husband and her son. *"Bonsoir, mes chers."* She kissed them both on the cheeks three times and then, before even taking off her coat, held up her pocketbook for them to see. "It is so heavy today I thought I would have to call one of you to come and help me carry it home." She laughed, took off her coat and began setting the table.

Pierre, his eyes twinkling, stole a glance at his son. "Jean Louis here thinks your pocketbook is just full of strange coins that are worthless. Perhaps you should have lightened your load by dropping some of them in the sewer."

Madam Mollet looked at her son and frowned. "Not on your life, Jean Louis! There are many coins in my pocketbook that are worth more than francs. You should go with your father to the bank tomorrow; then you would see how much they are worth." She continued setting the table. Jean Louis looked at her. "How long will it be before supper is ready? A new American film is playing at the cinema tonight."

Madam Mollet put her hands on her hips and laughed. "Your father says I am the best cook in all Provence. But even I cannot prepare a meal while I am guiding tourists around the *Palais.*" "I don't understand why you have to work at the *Palais*, Mama." "But I like to work there, Jean Louis." She put two thin loaves of bread on the table and then disappeared into the pantry. She returned carrying a wooden tray with an assortment of cold meats and cheeses. She put it in the middle of the table and sat down.

Pierre opened a bottle of wine and poured three glasses. He turned to his wife. So, it was a busy day at the *Palais, n'est pas?*"

Madam Mollet nodded. "Yes, very busy. But there were too many Germans." She frowned. "I do not like Germans; they are rude and arrogant. One would think they had won the war."

Jean Louis, about to help himself to the meat and cheese, stopped.

"They did, so far as France was concerned."

Pierre looked at his son, surprised. "How can you say such a thing?"

"Well, it's true, Papa, isn't it?"

Pierre thumped his fist on the table. "No, it is not true!"

"But, Papa, the whole country was —"

"Weaklings! *Petainists!* Traitors! Those of us who fought with the Free French never surrendered." He pointed his finger at his son. "And in the end, remember, it was we who were victorious, not the *Boche!*" Madam Mollet could see an argument developing. "Please, let's not talk about the war."

"But I want to talk about it, Mama. At least the war was a time when Papa was doing something important; not like now when he is just a —"

Madam Mollet let her knife and fork drop on the table with a clatter, and glared at her son to silence him. Pierre shrugged. "Let him go on. If it is something inside him, it is better it comes out," He turned to Jean Louis. "Go ahead, say what is on your mind."

"It is just that . . ." He hesitated. "I mean your job at the bank, Papa, my friends all say that —"

Madam Mollet again cut him off. "Your father has a very important job at the bank. Do you know that in all the years he has worked there, no one has tried to rob it."

"That's it, Mama, even if there were a robbery, Papa could not stop it; the bank does not even give him bullets for the gun he wears. My friends all make fun of him. They say he is there only for people to see, that he . . ." His eyes avoided his father's. ". . . that he is like the *Palais.*"

Madam Mollet threw up her arms. "That is foolishness!" She was angry now. "I forbid any more of such talk."

Jean Louis swallowed the rest of his wine, and pushed his chair back from the table. "I have to leave now; otherwise I will be late for the cinema." He looked at his mother for permission to leave, then got up and left.

Pierre finished his meal in silence. Madam Mollet cleared the table and took the dishes out to the pantry. She washed the dishes and returned to find her husband still sitting at the empty table staring at the wall. She was about to sit down with him when he stood up and walked into the living room. Her eyes followed him as he went to his desk, opened one of the drawers and took out a thin blue envelope. "I thought you said you had thrown that letter away. You said – "

He growled at her. "No, I did not throw it away."

"You said it would be madness to do what he suggests."

"I know what I said."

"But you are not thinking of responding to it?"

He turned and looked at her. "Jean Louis is right; if there were a robbery at the bank, I could not stop it; I would be useless." Madam Mollet laughed. "Now you are talking foolishness. Jean Louis is still a child; he is-"

"No, he is right. My job at the bank is a meaningless one. In a short time, I will be replaced by a television camera."

She got up from the table and walked over to him. She put her hand on his shoulder. *"Mon Cher*, in a few years you will be retired anyway."

He brushed her hand away. "Yes, retired! A sign I am too old to be useful for anything anymore!" He stormed across the room to the telephone. "And what then? What will I be able to say I have done with my life? Jean Louis is right." He began dialing.

Madam Mollet continued to protest. "You are being as foolish as Jean Louis. Hang up and we will talk."

He kept dialing. "There is no point in talking. I have made up my mind." He reached the person he was calling and spoke into the phone. "Hello. Jan? It is Pierre, Pierre Mollet. Yes, I received your letter; that is why I am calling. I have decided to accept. I will be there, yes, in the *Grand Place*, on the 30th." He hung up and turned to his wife. She was standing, her hands on her hips, shaking her head. He walked over to her and put his arms around her. "I've got to do it, Yvonne, it's my last chance to show our son that his father is more than just . . ." He paused. " . . . more than just a *Palais.*"

London, England, August 17, 1978 . . .

For as long as anyone could remember, Fenwick's firm had been the auditors for Lancaster Associates Ltd. No one could pinpoint when the relationship began but it was generally agreed it predated the Boer War. Since then, a succession of partners in the firm had looked after the account. Fenwick, the latest, had inherited it a year ago. He was on his way now by Underground to meet with his client and deliver the firm's report of its annual audit. He was not looking forward to the meeting. The report was one none of his predecessors ever had to deliver. As he dropped his 10p in the turnstile, the man in the change booth called out to him. "Not going to Moorgate, are you gov'nor?"

"As a matter of fact, I am."

The man shook his head. "Been a derailment at Baker Street; whole Tottenham Court Line is down."

Fenwick frowned. "That means I'll have to go around by way of Old Brompton Place."

"That's the way you'll have to go, gov'nor. And it'll take you longer than usual; trains have been slowed down throughout the whole system."

Fenwick pushed through the turnstile, walked down the slow moving escalator, and hurried along the tube tunnel to the platform for Kensington. The train had just pulled out. He cursed his bad luck; he'd never make it to Lancaster's office by nine. He considered going back upstairs and taking a bus but decided against it. It would take just as long, he told himself.

As he stood waiting for the next train, he looked down at his attaché case on the platform beside him. In it was the disastrous financial report he had prepared. He shook his head. No matter how he had tried to manipulate the figures, the picture remained clear: Lancaster Associates, Ltd, one of the oldest and most respected maritime brokerage houses in London was going under.

The problem, plain and simple, was Cecil Lancaster, the company's Managing Director. Lancaster, like Winston Churchill, was an intractable Victorian who stubbornly refused to accept that England was no longer and would never again be a world power. Every year since World War II his company, heavily dependent on British influence abroad, had lost money. Yet he persisted in maintaining the same lavish lifestyle the Lancasters before him all enjoyed. He brushed aside as rubbish Fenwick's advise that he sell his estate in Esher or his townhouse in Belgravia. The truth was he could no longer afford either.

A train was coming. Fenwick picked up his attaché case and stepped to the edge of the platform. The brushing aside was over. The figures Lancaster would see today would leave no doubt in his mind that financial disaster was now imminent.

"Good morning, Fenwick."

The voice, as usual, did not come from behind the heavy oak desk in the middle of the office. Fenwick would have been surprised if it had. He was accustomed to finding his client anywhere but sitting at his desk. He would expect to find him standing in one of the corners chipping golf balls into a whiskey tumbler, or in another corner, perched red-faced on his exercise bicycle, or even crouched behind the divan, shotgun in hand, practicing for the opening of the mallard season. More than once, Fenwick had arrived only to be motioned to one of the red leather chairs, to sit quietly and wait while Lancaster pondered his next move in an interminable game of chess he played by correspondence with the company's agent in Bombay. "Honor bound to record my time on the chess clock, old man," Lancaster would say without looking up. "Got the damn Sikh where I want him and I'm running out of time. If I make the wrong move now, I could end up with another bloody drawn game." Fenwick would wait patiently, having learned to accept his client's idiosyncrasies without complaint.

Idiosyncrasies were one thing; Lancaster's total lack of concern about his company's deteriorating financial condition was quite another. It was difficult enough trying to discuss serious business problems with a client dressed in golf knickers or a riding habit or full duck hunting regalia; but having him repeatedly dismiss those problems with a casual, "Well, you're the accountant, old man: I'm sure you can work it all out somehow," was becoming more than Fenwick could tolerate.

Surprisingly, today was different. Lancaster was dressed in a gray business suit and standing staring out the window, his hands clasped behind him, his thick John Bull face resting on his chest. He waved aside Fenwick's apology for being late. "I know, I know, the derailment: I heard about it on the wireless. Rather nasty accident, they said, several people badly injured. It's that sharp turn at Baker Street. They'll have the usual investigation and end up blaming the conductor. But it's that bloody turn; it should have been fixed years ago." He looked at Fenwick. "Well, don't just stand there, old man; get out that dreadful report you want to give me. And don't bother with all that accounting mumble jumble; just tell me how bad it is."

Fenwick took out the report he had brought. "About as bad as it could be, I'm afraid. The critical figures are here in the agency accounts that have not been paid. Two of them, Midland and Imperial, are demanding immediate payment. I'm afraid it's just a matter of time until – "

"How much do we owe them?"

Femwick looked at the figures. "Midland, over sixty thousand pounds; Imperial, nearly as much." He handed the report to Lancaster. "Even if you liquidated everything, you would not be able to pay them. There is no alternative; you will have to file a declaration of voluntary bankruptcy."

"And if I don't file such a declaration?"

"You really have no choice. If you don't file, Midland or Imperial will file to have you adjudged involuntarily."

Lancaster turned and stared out the window again. For several minutes, he did not say anything. Then he broke the silence with a question. "How much time do I have?"

"Now that you've been given the figures, you really should file the declaration straightaway. I have brought the necessary papers for you to sign."

Lancaster shook his head. His accountant had not understood his question. "No, I mean how long before we can expect Midland or Imperial to do something?"

"Surely, you're not thinking of waiting until – "

Lancaster interrupted him. "Suppose I made a good faith payment to both of them, giving my word in an affidavit that the rest will be forthcoming shortly. That would keep them from filing anything for a while, wouldn't it?

"Yes, but you can't make a promise like that. And in an affidavit! You would be inviting a criminal proceeding for fraud when they did file their petitions."

Lancaster brushed aside the objection. "Look, old man, I know how I can get the money, all of it. But I need time. He pointed to the report in Fenwick's hand. "And the money I'm talking about isn't in those bloody figures of yours. I can't say any more about it, just that I can get it." He paused. "But I need time."

Fenwick was skeptical. "How would you even make the good faith payments? They would have to be substantial, and you simply do not have the money."

"I do in the tax account."

Fenwick threw up his arms in protest. "Now you are adding tax fraud!"

Lancaster repeated his question. "How much time would I have?"

"As your accountant, I really must object."

"Yes, yes, I understand all of that; just tell me how long you think I could keep Midland and Imperial at bay."

"Well, if you insist." Fenwick continued to grumble under his breath. "Good faith payments, if they were substantial, would probably discourage them from doing anything right away. How long they would ultimately wait is impossible to say." He paused and added sardonically: "They would, of course, be influenced by the fact that Lancaster Associates Ltd. Has always enjoyed a reputation for –"

"And my willingness to provide an affidavit?"

Fenwick agreed, begrudgingly, "Yes"

"So what's the bottom line? How much time would I have?"

Fenwick thought for a moment. "Sixty days, perhaps ninety."

Lancaster's face broke into a broad smile. "Two months!

Maybe even three!" He laughed. "That's more than enough time for what I have to do."

Fenwick had no idea what his client was talking about. He decided to try again to reason with him. "I really must point out that it is my duty as your accountant to advise against any action that –" He stopped. Lancaster was no longer listening to him. He had gone to the coat closet and was looking for something. He found it and turned to Fenwick. "Say, old man, would you mind terribly moving back a bit. I've just bought this new nine iron and really should practice chipping with it.

Fenwick had only been gone a few minutes and Lancaster's office looked like a practice green, golf balls strewn everywhere, more than a dozen clustered around an upturned hat on the spot where his accountant had been standing.

Lancaster used his nine iron to poke another ball into position between his feet. Then, with a short crisp swing of the club, he sent the ball flying across the room. It missed the hat, struck the leg of a chair and rolled under the library table. He chipped a few more balls and then walked over to the hat. He counted his successes, and shrugged. He put away the golf club and sat down at his desk. The top of his desk was bare except for a pipe rack containing an assortment of pipes, all Meerschaums. He selected one of the pipes, filled it with a coarse dark tobacco, and lit it with a silver lighter. He took several puffs, then sat back in his chair, rubbed the bowl of the pipe against the palm of his hand, and smiled. Lancasters had always smoked Meerschaums, he reminded himself, it had been a family tradition dating back to the time his great grandfather was given one by the Empress Dowager of China during her fragile peace with England during the Opium wars.

He received his first Meerschaum on his eighteenth birthday. He remembered the day clearly. It was the day in 1940 that he reported to Aldershot to begin special training for the new "Commando" unit the army was forming to make hit and run attacks at night on the occupied French coast. He sat smoking his pipe, thinking back to his experiences during the war, something he had not done in years - that is, until a week ago. He spun his chair around, unlocked the cabinet of his credenza, and took out a small metal box. He put the box on his desk and opened it. In it was the thin blue envelope he had received last week from *The Hague.*

Maduradam, Netherlands, August 20, 1978 . . .

Osterbeek finished writing the quarterly report for the Manager of *The Hague* office to send to the Board of Directors in Rotterdam. He initialed it and threw it in his outbox. For twelve years he had been writing the Manager's reports for him. This was the last one he would have to write. The company had been sold to a Japanese conglomerate, *The Hague* office was being closed, and everyone in it was being declared redundant.

Under other circumstances, he might have challenged his redundancy, even contested the matter in court to protest publicly another surrender by the Dutch to a former enemy whose wartime atrocities they still had not forgiven. But he was not going to challenge his redundancy in court or otherwise. His reason was simple: it a short time, if he played his cards right, he would be one of the richest men in Holland.

He lit his third cigar of the day and sat back in chair to review what still had to be done. The first thing was the meeting today with Grappi at *Maduradam*. The fat little Monsignor would be pompous as always but they would both know he was there simply as a messenger to agree to Osterbeek's demand.

After *Maduradam,* the next step was the meeting in Brussels with Lancaster and Mollet, both of whom had now agreed to join in the plan. Finally, there was the matter of the Major's young widow, a delicate matter that had to be handled carefully. He frowned. It was still possible she was telling the truth about the sonata. He opened the desk drawer, took out the notes of his telephone conversation with her, and studied them. No, he was certain she knew and could play it. He continued to study the notes. It was also clear that she did not know what happened in Italy, that the Major had kept that from her. Perfect, he told himself; she will be curious and want him to tell her. He took several puffs on his cigar and blew a thick cloud of smoke up at the ceiling. He smiled. He will tell her what happened. Yes, he will tell her everything, changing the story only slightly – just enough to persuade her to play the sonata for him.

It was twilight and the small park was deserted. The afternoon crowd had gone and it was too early for the evening flood of visitors. A uniformed attendant strolled leisurely from one exhibit to the next switching on the tiny lights in the miniature houses and along the miniature streets and canals that made up the Lilliputian world of Maduradam. The knee-high replicas of Amsterdam, *Gouda, Horne* and dozens of other quaint Dutch cities and towns began twinkling in the dusk. In the Amsterdam exhibit, a tiny *Rondvaart* boat was approaching a small bridge in front of the dollhouse sized *Rijksmuseum.* It was about to pass under it when a giant hand reached down and turned it sideways. Behind it, the water in the canal, unable to flow through the little arched opening, began rising. The hand belonged to Osterbeek who had just hunkered down by the exhibit, interrupting his conversation with the man he was standing beside. "We have talked long enough, Monsignor; I am losing my patience in this matter."

Monsignor Grappi smiled down at him condescendingly. "Do not misunderstand me; I am not denying His Eminence's interest in the document. It is just that the price you ask is out of the question."

Osterbeek was still holding the little *Rondvaart* boat pressed against the bridge. The rising water was slowly covering his hand. "It is time to end the pretense, Monsignor; the Cardinal would not have sent you here if he was not prepared to accept my offer."

Grappi stopped smiling. It was time, he decided, to use the veiled threat he had been saving. He put his hand on Osterbeek's shoulder. "I feel it is only fair to tell you, Herr Osterbeek, that his Eminence has initiated efforts of his own to find the document. If he finds it without your help, you will of course end up with nothing."

Osterbeek responded with a derisive laugh. "Your Cardinal can initiate whatever efforts he wishes; the document is hidden where he would not find it in a thousand years."

The little Rondvaart boat was now completely submerged in the water rising in the canal. Grappi pointed to it. "Why are you doing that?"

Osterbeek looked up at him. "Because I am through haggling with you. Watch the water closely. It has almost risen to the top of the canal. When it does and overflows, my offer to your Cardinal will expire. We will have nothing further so say to one another. I will leave and make arrangements to sell the document to others I know will be interested in obtaining it."

The rising water now covered all of Osterbeek's hand. It reached the top of the canal and a tiny stream trickled out into the miniature street beside it. Osterbeek kept the submerged boat pressed against the bridge. The water began overflowing both sides of the canal.

Grappi cleared his throat. "His Eminence will have to know the number of the account in Switzerland."

Osterbeek let the boat slip under the bridge and out the other side. The head of water behind it rushed through the opening sending it yawing down the canal toward the *Rotterdam* exhibit.

Osterbeek stood up. He dried his hand on the sleeve of his jacket. He took a small white card with a number written on it out of his pocket. He handed the card to Grappi. "The entire sum is to be deposited before the document will be delivered." He turned and walked away.

Grappi stood for a moment looking down at the Amsterdam exhibit. The water in the canal was now flowing normally again, another little *Rondvaart* boat approaching the bridge in front of the *Rijksmuseum.*

Brookline, Massachusetts, August 21, 1978 . . .

It was another bad toss; the ball did not go high enough. Cathy let it drop on the court, caught it on the bounce, and threw it up again. She arched her back and served. The ball went into the net and then dribbled over to where Biancalana was playing as her doubles partner. He poked the ball off the court with his racket. He glanced over his Shoulder at her. "C'mon, Cathy, you're a good server; get the next one in. Let's fight our way back to deuce." The next serve was long, a double fault that ended the match. Cathy dropped her racket in disgust. "Well, I sure blew that game!" She picked up her racket and ran to the net where their opponents were waiting to shake hands. "Too bad, Cathy, that was a tough way to lose the set. Do you want to play another?"

Cathy shook her head. "I'd like to quit if you don't mind."

Their opponents smiled politely. "We understand."

The afternoon sun had slipped behind the roof of the clubhouse and the wide veranda where Cathy and Joe were sitting was now all in shade. Biancalana had finished his gin and tonic and was rattling the ice cubes around the bottom of his glass. "What's the matter, Cathy; you haven't said three words since we came up from the courts?"

"I'm sorry, Joe, I know my game was dreadful."

"Aw, you were just having an off day; we all have them. Something else is bothering you, I can tell. What is it?"

"It's just that I can't stop thinking about that telephone call."

Biancalana was surprised. "You don't mean the one from that guy in Holland?"

Cathy nodded. "Yes. He said he was with Charles during the war and had something important to tell me, something about the notes of the sonata that Charles could play."

Biancalana frowned. "I thought we decided the guy was some kind of nut and that –"

Cathy shook her head. "No, I don't think he is, Joe. Why would he make up a story like that? No, I think he's telling the truth." She looked at Biancalana. "And you know what that means, Joe; it means he knows what happened in Italy, that Charles would never –"

Biancalana did not let her finish. He stood up, turned his back on her, and stormed over to the edge of the veranda. He leaned out over the railing, looking down on the courts below, muttering to himself. "There they are, Noonan and his spouse-equivalent, or whatever you want to call her, practicing again. The bastards are really out to beat us this year." Cathy sat there playing with the straw in her empty glass, surprised at his reaction to what she had said.

Biancalana continued muttering and then suddenly turned about and looked at her, his face red with anger. "You know what I think?"

"What?"

"That you'll never hear from that Dutch nut again. I'd be willing to bet you twenty bucks that –"

Cathy laughed. "You'd lose the bet, Joe."

"Oh yeah? Why?"

"Because he's coming over."

"What?"

"I agreed to meet with him."

"You didn't tell me that!"

"He asked me not to say anything to anyone, even about his telephone call, until he had a chance to explain everything to me."

Biancalana's Italian temper erupted and he kicked the railing. "Thanks! Thanks a lot! Not only do you agree to meet with this nut; you agree to keep it a secret from me. Thanks a lot!"

Cathy, accustomed to Biancalana's outbursts of temper, smiled. "Now you're mad at me."

Biancalana kicked the railing again. "Why the hell shouldn't I be?"

Cathy tried to placate him. "Come on, Joe, it's not a big deal. And I didn't agree to keep it a secret from you. I told you about the telephone call, didn't I?" She tried to coax him back to the table. "Come on, come back and sit down. I want to talk to you about it."

Biancalana just stood there, leaning against the railing, his face redder than ever. Cathy got up and walked over to him. She put her hand on his arm. "Joe, you know when I married Charles how everyone thought it wouldn't work, but it did. The reason it did was because we were always open with each other about everything. That's why this whole thing about the sonata has always been such a mystery to me. And when Charles died, I thought it would stay a mystery forever, always be a part of his life I never knew about. Then, out of the blue, this fellow Osterbeek calls me and says he was with Charles in Italy, and knows all about the sonata. Don't you see, Joe, now I've got a chance to –"

Biancalana pulled away from her arm. "No, I don't see. What if there is a part of his life you don't know about? So what? That was forty years ago; it's ancient history. The Judge may have been a great guy; I'm not saying he wasn't. But we've already given him enough of our lives. And we both know that even if he didn't have that stroke, we'd have –"

Cathy cut him off. "We don't know that, Joe; we don't know what we'd have done. It didn't happen that way, so we don't know what we would have done." She put her hand on his arm again. "All we know is how we feel about each other now. That's really all that matters."

Biancalana pulled away again. "If that's all that matters, why can't you forget about what the Judge did during the war? He's dead now; you're not married to him anymore. All the time he was in a wheelchair, when he wasn't even a person anymore, we still felt guilty every time we made love. Now he's gone and you're still trying to stay married to a part of him."

Cathy frowned. "You don't understand, Joe. It's just something I've always wanted to know about. I don't see why you have to think that –"

Biancalana cut her off. "Look, it's obvious you've made up your mind, so what the hell difference does it make what I think?"

Cathy had had enough. She walked back to her chair, lifted her sweater off the back of it, and started for the clubhouse. "I thought you'd understand, but I can see I was wrong."

Biancalana watched her walk away. He waited until she had reached the door and then yelled to her. "So when is this Dutch nut of yours coming over anyway?"

She threw the answer back over her shoulder without turning around. "A week from today, on the thirty-first."

Biancalana banged his fist on the table. "Great! That's the day before we have to qualify for the tournament. You'll probably play even lousier than you did today." Cathy did not hear him. She had already disappeared into the clubhouse.

Brussels, Belgium, August 28, 1978 . . . The outdoor cafes in Brussels' *Grand Place* were overflowing with early evening patrons, laughing and joking over their drinks and honing their appetites for the restaurants on the nearby *Rue de Bouchers.* In one of the cafes, *Le Charleroi,* Mollet and Lancaster were sitting waiting.

Mollet was getting impatient. "He's late; he said six o'clock."

Lancaster took out his meerschaum. "Relax, Pierre, it's only a bit after that. He'll be here, don't worry." He pointed with his pipe out over the large square. "There, I think I see him coming now." He was right. Osterbeek was threading his way through the crowd towards them. The Dutchman reached *Le Charleroi*, stopped briefly to speak to the maitre d', and then hurried over to join them at the table.

The three men had not seen each other in more than forty years and reminisced about their experiences together during the war while they waited for the maitre d'to bring the bottle of wine Osterbeek had ordered. The maitre d' arrived, filled their glasses and left. Their conversation then turned to the purpose of the meeting. Osterbeek proposed a toast. "To us, three former comrades-in-arms who before long will all be rich beyond our wildest dreams." He tapped his glass against Lancaster's and Mollet's. "I can now report to you that the Vatican has made the deposit in the escrow account in Switzerland. All that remains is for us to produce the document and the money is ours!"

Mollet was the first to ask a question. "Are we certain the document is still there?"

Osterbeek nodded. "Yes, I went there to make sure." He leaned over the table, lowered his voice, and told them of his visit to the abbey.

"So the document is still in the crypt buried under - "

" - under some of the rubble of the explosion, yes."

Lancaster poked his Meerschaum into the conversation. "That means we'll have to dig our way down to the door."

"Yes, it will take a few hours of digging, at night when we know the old priest will not be there." Osterbeek anticipated their next question. "And yes, the organ is still there in the chapel, and is in working condition. I made certain of that too." Lancaster and Mollet continued to pepper him with questions:

"We don't understand this whole Concordat business. Why were the signatures torn off the original?"

"Yes, and why did Franco have them?"

"And why a forgery? Who prepared it? Was it –"

Osterbeek laughed and held up his hand. "Wait, wait; you are putting too many questions to me at once. Give me a chance and I will try to answer all of them." He sat back in his chair and took out a cigar. He lit it, took several puffs on it, and then blew a cloud of smoke out over the low hedge separating them from the crowded square. He leaned forward again over the table and related what happened in Rome.

Mollet and Lancaster waited until he had finished telling them about his meeting with Borielli, and then asked another question. "You say that when you left the old Cardinal you were confident you would hear from him again . Did you?"

Osterbeek smiled. "Yes, a week or so later, after I had returned to Holland. I received a call from Grappi. He said he was in *The Hague*. He pretended he was there on other business and was calling me simply to find out if I had changed my mind about discussing with him the serious allegations I had made. I knew he was lying, that he had been sent to The Hague specifically to meet with me and arrange to obtain the document. I met with him and let him pretend otherwise. I wanted to satisfy myself that the Cardinal had the authority to transfer large sums of money from the Vatican treasury. When I was satisfied on that score, I brought the meeting to an end, threatening to sell the document elsewhere. As I expected, he capitulated and said I would receive the amount I was demanding. I waited until the money was transferred to the Swiss account, and then communicated with both of you."

Mollet saw that the bottle of wine was empty and signaled the waiter to bring another. "You have told us about the abbey and about this Cardinal Borielli. You have not told us anything about the major's widow. In your letter, you said you had communicated with her."

Osterbeek nodded. "I telephone her right after my meeting with Grappi. I had already made some discrete inquiries about her but did not want to communicate with her until I had settled the matter with Borielli."

"You mentioned that she is a pianist."

The Dutchman smiled. "That was a stroke of luck I had not anticipated. "As it turns out, she is quite accomplished."

Lancaster and Mollet both asked the same question. "But does she know the notes to the sonata?"

"I am convinced she does."

"What did you say to her?"

Osterbeek took several puffs on his cigar. "Well, first of all, I pretended to know nothing about the Major's death. I even had the call placed to him. When she took it, I introduced myself as an old comrade who had served with him in the war. I expressed shock at hearing he had died, and extended my condolences. I said I was calling because something had come up relating to when her late husband and I were trapped together behind enemy lines in Italy. I said it was something I felt she would want to know about."

"What did she say?"

"She just listened. I related to her what happened in Italy, not everything to be sure, but enough to establish my creditability in the event the Major had told her anything."

"Had he?"

"I don't think so, at least not very much. She said he would never talk about it." Osterbeek smiled. "That, of course was what I was counting on, that Italy was a gap in his past she would be curious about."

Mollet frowned. "What did you tell her about Italy?"

Osterbeek knocked the ash off his cigar. "I told her the four of us were sent on a special mission behind the enemy lines in Italy, that the mission failed because our plane was shot down. I said we parachuted to safety and made our way to an old abbey where we hid from the Germans. I said that while we were at the abbey something occurred that none of us understood at the time, but which has now been explained by a recent, seemingly unrelated, event. I told her it was all too complicated to go into over the telephone but that it had to do with the notes to a sonata one of the monks at the abbey taught her husband to play." Lancaster coughed. "You were skating pretty close to the thin ice, weren't you?" Osterbeek nodded. "Yes, but I felt I had to stay close to the truth to avoid contradicting something the Major may have told her. I said we were all captured by the Germans and interned in a prison camp in Poland where we agreed to keep secret what happened at the abbey." He paused and drew on his cigar. "That's the end of what I told her. When I finished, she asked me what she could do. I said I was certain the Major had shown her the notes to the sonata and that -"

Mollet interrupted, "You were gambling at that point?"

"Yes." Osterbeek blew another cloud of smoke out over the hedge. "But I could tell from her response that I was right. I said when I had the notes to the sonata I would be in a position to obtain a very large sum of money, and that her share, because she was the Major's widow, would be half a million dollars." "What did she say to that?"

Osterbeek responded to their question by picking up his glass and holding it out over the middle of the table. "She agreed to meet with me; I am flying to the United States the day after tomorrow." He waited for Lancaster and Mollet to hold up their glasses. Then he tapped his against theirs. "To the three of us. By this time next week, old comrades, we will have the sonata."

Brookline, Massachusetts, August 30, 1978 ... Cathy and Joe were standing in front of the Tournament Board looking at the brackets of the pairings. Their first two matches would be pieces of cake, against unseeded opponents. The third match they would come up against another seeded team and the real competition would begin. Biancalana was grumbling about their not being the number one seed. "I still say we got screwed. We're the defending champions; we should have been seeded first, not Noonan."

Cathy shrugged. "I don't know, Joe, we haven't been playing well at all lately. And Ed and Marge have looked awfully good out there."

"Oh, bullshit! We'll beat their asses off in the final – if they can even get that far."

Cathy could see that Biancalana was in a bad mood. She decided, as she drove him home, to substitute music for conversation. She slipped a Neil Diamond concert into the tape deck. Diamond was in the middle of September Morn. When he finished they were at Biancalana's condominium. Cathy pulled over to the curb and stopped. "Joe?"

"What?"

"I wish you'd change your mind."

"About coming to your house?"

"Yes. I just want you to meet him, that's all."

"You mean, then I should leave."

Cathy frowned. "You know that's not what I mean. I promised him I'd talk to him alone, but that doesn't mean –"

Biancalana got out, slammed the door and walked away.

As Cathy swung into her driveway, she felt a tingle of excitement. At last, after all the years of wondering what happened in Italy and why Charles was so mysterious about the sonata he had learned there, now, finally, she was going to find out. She slid out of the car and hurried across the lawn to the front door. Her housekeeper was standing there holding the door open for her. "He's here, Mrs. Parkman. He just arrived a few minutes ago. I showed him into the living room."

Osterbeek was standing by one of the windows looking out. Cathy crossed the room with her hand extended. "Hi, I'm Cathy Parkman. Sorry I'm late."

Osterbeek smiled as he shook her hand. "I was admiring your lovely garden. That handsome tree in the middle is a maple, is it not?"

"Yes, a Norway Maple. It is almost a hundred years old. It makes a lovely bower to sit under on a hot day like this. Why don't we go out there and have our talk. I'll ask Martha to bring some iced tea – or would you prefer something stronger?"

"No, iced tea will be just fine, thank you."

They walked out through the French Doors into the garden. They spent a few minutes looking at the different flowerbeds, and then settled into two of the lawn chairs under the big maple. The housekeeper brought them a tray with two tall glasses of iced tea on it. She put it on the small table between them and left.

Cathy handed one of the glasses to Osterbeek, then took the other and sat back in her chair. "I'm anxious to hear everything you can tell me about Charles's experiences during the war. He would never talk about them."

Osterbeek nodded. "Your husband was a fine officer, Mrs. Parkman, liked and respected by everyone who served with him. I first met him in 1943 when we were picked, along with others, for a special mission behind the enemy lines in Italy." He took a sip of his tea and then told her all about Operation Bisect, explaining how it was supposed to shorten the war in Italy and describing how it failed because the Allies kept their troops too long at Anzio and allowed the Germans to move their army north to Rome. He finished his explanation and sat back in his chair. "As things turned out, our mission would have been irrelevant even if our plane had not been shot down and we had not had to parachute before we reached our drop zone. It was not long after we landed that the Germans captured us. We spent the rest of the war in one of their prison camps."

Cathy was disappointed. She was expecting more. "Yes, Charles told me all about how his mission failed, and how he ended up in a prison camp. He said the conditions were terrible." She looked at Osterbeek, trying to smile politely. "But what I'm really interested in is what happened before you were captured. I know something happened then, something he would never tell me about. I tried to get him to tell me but he wouldn't." She leaned forward in her chair. "But you were there; you know what happened; you can tell me."

Osterbeek put his glass back on the little table. "Yes, I was there. I can tell you what happened." He paused. "And when I do, I think you will understand why your husband was reluctant to talk about it." Cathy felt a tingle of excitement. "It's just that it's a part of his life I don't know a single thing about."

"Except for the sonata."

Cathy avoided Osterbeek's eyes by taking a sip of her tea. She hesitated, and then looked at him. "Yes, but I would never even have known about that if I hadn't come home one night and found him at the piano playing it. I asked him what it was, and how on earth he had learned to play it." Osterbeek leaned forward. "What did he say?"

"Only that it had to do with some old monks, and that it was better I didn't know anything more about it."

Osterbeek smiled. "Forgive me for sounding so inquisitive. I did not come here to ask questions; I came to tell you what happened." He paused. "I have to warn you, however, that the tale is a strange one. But when you have heard it, you will understand everything, including why I have come to see you." He reached in his pocket and took out a large cigar. "I am a cigar smoker. Do you mind if I have one here in your garden?"

Cathy shook her head. "No, go ahead; I don't mind at all."

Osterbeek lit the cigar, took several puffs on it and then settled back again in his chair. He proceeded to tell Cathy the whole story of the night her husband was summoned to the Abbot's study. Cathy was on the edge of her chair, listening to every word. "So that's why Charles felt he should keep the sonata a secret."

Osterbeek nodded. "Yes, and if it were not for the discovery I made recently, it would have remained a secret forever." He paused. "But I am getting ahead of my story. Let me go back to when we were in the wine cellar." He took several more puffs on his cigar and blew the smoke up into the leaves of the tree over their heads. "We had been hiding in the wine cellar for almost a week when the Germans came, a whole battalion, part of a Panzer division moving up from the south. The monks were all out in the vineyard, too far from the chapel to help us. Your husband had been spending every night with the Abbot learning the notes of the sonata." Osterbeek paused and smiled. "The time had come for his debut. He left the wine cellar and rushed up to the chapel. Lancaster, Mollet and I gathered up everything that might give us away, and hurried to where behind the stone steps, the door to the secret room was supposed to be. When we got there, we did not see any door, only a stone wall. We stood there wondering if the Abbot had made up the whole story for some reason. Then suddenly a section of the wall moved out and we could see that it was a door.' He smiled. "Your husband had done it! We waited for him to join us, then all of us slipped into the secret room, pulling the door closed behind us. The room we found ourselves in was a crypt. There were no windows and no other doors; it was like being in a vault. But there was an airshaft and we all gathered around that. Through it we could hear the German tanks and half-tracks rumbling by above us. The noise seemed to go on for an eternity. We sat there on the floor hoping they would keep on going and not stop at the abbey." He paused and took a sip of his tea. "It was while we were sitting there that we noticed a small iron chest in one of the corners of the crypt. We were curious what it contained, so we went over and opened it. All it contained was an old document that we could see was handwritten in both Spanish and Latin. The bottom of the last page was torn off and missing. Your husband and the others went back to the airshaft and sat down again. I continued to study the document. Written sometime in the early 1940s, it appeared to be a religious appeal to General Franco to save the Spanish Jews from Hitler's anti-Semitic programs. I concluded that it was probably something one of the monks had written. I threw it back in the iron chest, and joined your husband and the others. We could tell from the sounds coming down the airshaft that the Germans were not leaving, and that even more were coming. We felt we were safe in the crypt, but we had no food or water and we knew we could not stay there indefinitely. Two days passed and our situation worsened. By the third day, we were desperate. We decided, whatever the risk, we had to try to escape. We waited until the middle of the night and then made a run for it. We didn't have a chance; the Germans were everywhere. We were caught before we could even get to the vineyard. The soldiers who captured us wanted to shoot us on the spot, but we were still in uniform and so they had to treat us as prisoners of war. The monks we not so lucky. They were civilian and had harbored the enemy. The Germans lined them all up against the wall of the abbey and machine gunned them."

Cathy shuttered. "That must have been terrible."

"Yes, and there was nothing we could do but watch. The Germans then blew up the building where the monks lived, burying the wine cellar and the crypt under a pile of rubble. It turned out they were not planning to stay as we thought. The next day, the whole Panzer division pulled out to get to Rome before the Allies." He shook his head. "Ironically, if we had remained hidden in the crypt one more day, the Germans would have been gone and the monks' lives spared."

Cathy leaned forward. "I think I can understand now why Charles did not want to talk about it."

Osterbeek nodded. "Yes, but that was many years ago. And I would not be dredging it up now if it were not for the recent event I mentioned to you." He smiled. "Tell me, do you believe in coincidences?"

Cathy laughed. "Sometimes, why?"

"Because what I am about to tell you involved a remarkable one. To appreciate how remarkable, you have to understand that I am a confirmed creature of habit, addicted to the same routine every day." He took a sip of his tea. "Each morning, I walk to the station in the small town where I live and catch the 7:02 train to *The Hague* where I work. I buy the morning newspaper at the station, glance through it on the train, and leave it for the conductor when I get off. I say 'glance through it' because, although I read the major news items, the journey to *The Hague* is brief and does not permit more than a perusal of the rest of the paper. Rarely do I take note of anything in the back pages." He could see that Cathy was beginning to wonder what all of this had to do with the abbey in Italy. He paused and smiled. "I apologize for what must seem a boring recital of my morning commute, but it has a bearing on the rest of the story."

Cathy smiled. "I was sure it did. Please go on."

Osterbeek took several puffs on his cigar. "The 7:02 is very reliable. In all the years I have taken it, it has never failed to arrive in *The Hague* on time. This particular day, however, it was delayed because a band of Malaccans had put a wooden barrier across the tracks to protest the government's policy on Indonesia. Removal of the barrier took almost an hour, during which we had to sit in the train and wait. Because of the delay, I had time to read the morning paper from beginning to end. The last page contained a small article that, had it not been for the Malaccans, I would have missed."

"The coincidence?"

"Yes, Franco had recently died, and the article reported that his personal effects included a curious item no one could explain: a piece of paper that appeared to have been torn from some important document and bore only the signature of Pope Pius XII and the date May 12, 1941. The article went on to say that a search had been made for the missing document but it was not among Franco's effects."

Cathy gasped. "The document in the crypt!"

Osterbeek nodded. "I was certain it was. I suddenly realized the enormous significance of what I knew. Since World War II, rumors have persisted that Pius XII was anti-Semitic, that he even endorsed Hitler's persecution of the Jews. The document in the crypt was an impassioned plea to Franco to protect the Spanish Jews from such persecution. It was a clear refutation of those rumors." He knocked the ash off his cigar. "As soon as my train reached *The Hague*, I telephoned the Madrid paper and spoke to the person who wrote the article. He told me the piece of paper had been turned over to the Vatican but they had no record of any document to match it. I asked him to describe the piece of paper for me. He said it contained the Pope's signature, which the Vatican verified as genuine, and the date May 12, 1941, that's all. I asked him if the date was in the same handwriting as the signature." "Was it?"

Osterbeek looked at her and smiled. "He said it was very different, that the date was written in an unusual elaborate script."

Cathy felt another tinge of excitement. "But do we know the document itself still exists?"

"Yes, I went back to the abbey to make certain." He told Cathy about his trip there and what he had learned.

"So, it is still there, buried under the rubble?"

"Yes." Osterbeek paused to re-light his cigar and then continued. "When I returned from the abbey, I sent a note, through a discreet channel, to the Vatican. My note said simply that the mysterious piece of paper bearing Pope Pius XII's signature had been torn from a document of great historical significance, and that I knew where the document was."

"What response did you get?"

Osterbeek blew another cloud of smoke up into the maple tree. "What I expected: the Vatican was skeptical. I received a pro forma letter from some underling asking me to submit my information I had about the missing document."

"What did you do?"

"I ignored the letter and waited."

"And then –?"

Osterbeek smiled. "A short time later I was visited by a local priest who said he had been instructed to investigate my claim. I gave him a very general description of the missing document but refused to say anything more except to a member of the Curia. He tried to squeeze more information out of me but I was adamant. He left, promising only to report what I had told him to his superiors. It was not long before I was visited again, this time by a Monsignor from Rome. He said he had been sent by one of the Cardinals there. I told him what

I had told the priest, adding a little but not much. He asked me a litany of questions, most of which I refused to answer. He finally got around to asking how much I expected to receive for the document. I looked him straight in the eye. I told him I did not intend to haggle over the price, that I would deliver the document to the Vatican for two million dollars and nothing less," Cathy's eyes widened. "What did he say to that?"

"That my demand was preposterous, that his Cardinal would decide what the document was worth, if anything. I just laughed, said it was obvious we had nothing further to say to each other, and he left."

"But that was not the end of it?"

"No. Less than a week later, I received a telephone call from Rome. It was the Monsignor again. He said I was to come to the Vatican, that his Cardinal was prepared to meet with me." Osterbeek smiled. "I knew then that I had won. If the Vatican intended to negotiate further, they would have used the Monsignor; their willingness to have a Cardinal meet with me was a clear sign that the Vatican was prepared to pay what I was demanding for the document."

" – Which you did not have."

Osterbeek nodded. "True. The time had come to involve your husband and the others. When I learned that your husband had died, I asked Lancaster and Mollet to meet me in Brussels so we could decide what to do. The three of us met and agreed that I should come and see you."

"Because of the sonata."

"That was one reason, yes. Our plan is to go to the abbey at night, dig down to the door of the crypt, and -"

Cathy interrupted him. "You said the sonata was one reason; there was another?"

"Yes. When the three of us met in Brussels, we considered the possibility you did not know the notes to the sonata and could not help us. We decided, in that event, to proceed with an alternative plan, opening the door with an explosive. This would increase the risk of discovery, but we agreed to do it nonetheless. We also agreed that, whether you knew the notes or not, you were entitled, as the Major's widow, to share with us the two million dollars that . . . " He paused and smiled " . . . that I can now report to you the Vatican has deposited in an escrow account for us in Switzerland."

It was getting cooler in the garden. The sun, still bright, was losing its warmth. Osterbeek told Cathy he had finished his story. He settled back in his chair, puffing what was left of his cigar and watching the afternoon breeze rustle through the leaves of the maple.

Cathy put on her sweater. For several minutes, neither of them said anything. Cathy broke the silence.

"You won't need to use an explosive."

Osterbeek smiled. "Good. You have only to write down the notes for me and –"

"That won't be necessary either."

"I don't understand."

Cathy looked at him. "I've decided to go with you to the abbey."

Brookline, Massachusetts, September 4, 1978 . . . Tradition called for all championship matches to be played on the Clubhouse Court, the oldest and at one time only court at Longwood. This was no problem in the early years when membership was small and everyone could comfortably watch the matches from the spacious clubhouse veranda.

But as membership grew, the veranda became inadequate for the large crowds of spectators, and portable stands had to be added to preserve the old tradition.

Today was like a throwback to the old days. The temperature was over ninety, the portable stands were nearly empty, and almost everyone was crowded up on the veranda in the protective shade of its overhanging roof.

Down on the court, the players were taking a five-minute break before beginning the third and decisive set. Cathy and Joe, the defending champions, had barely squeaked out a win in the first set, then lost the second one when Biancalana, normally a strong server, double-faulted twice in a tie-breaker.

Cathy had flopped down on one of the player's chairs, and was toweling the perspiration off her arms and legs. She glanced at Biancalana on the chair beside her. He had his head turned the other way, avoiding looking at her. She frowned; he was still mad at her. The night before last, when she telephoned him and told him she was going to Italy, he had hung up on her. They had hardly spoken since. "Time!" The umpire perched in his high green chair at center court signaled for play to resume. Biancalana stood up. He started out on the court and then turned and looked back at Cathy. "I want you to know I think this whole thing you're doing about the Judge's past is just a big guilt trip, that's all."

Cathy frowned. "Guilt about what?" The anger bottle up inside Biancalana poured out. "I don't know, maybe about sleeping with me when he was still alive and couldn't do it. Or maybe – "

She did not let him finish. She gave him an icy look and walked away from him back out on the court. The third set was disappointing to the spectators. The defending champions played poorly, winning only one game. After the final point, they shook hands with the new champions, and then hurried away separately toward the locker rooms.

The Vatican, September 6, 1978 . . .

Borielli's faith in Grappi had been restored. After almost three years of hearing nothing but frustrating reports of fruitless searches, his loyal Monsignor had at last come up with something. It was not where the missing Concordat was hidden; he was still in the dark about that. But he had learned from his sources that the Dutchman and three accomplices were coming to Italy to recover it, that they had booked rooms at the Hotel DaVinci in Florence for the 15th and 16th of September and had seats on the first flight from Rome to Geneva the day after. He had also learned of an unusual visit the Dutchman had made earlier to an old abandoned abbey in nearby *Valdarno,* which suggested the document was hidden there. Borielli rubbed his thin hands together and smiled to himself. The escrow account with the Swiss Bank stipulated that if the document was not produced within a month, the entire sum in the account was to be returned to the Vatican. This meant that now he would be able to get the document without paying a single lire for it. And there would be no witnesses left to blackmail him later.

VillaD'Est, Rome, September 7, 1978 . . .

The spectacular beauty of Rome's *VillaD'Est* is enhanced by the knowledge that the force creating the hundreds of fountains there, some spurting higher than a ten-story building, is simply gravity, harnessed by the Romans in an ingenious system of underground pipes and valves designed nine centuries ago. So well is the system designed that even today, the fountains still flow in perfect harmony, surrounding modern day visitors, as it did their Roman counterparts, with the relaxing sound of gently gurgling water.

The man walking beside Monsignor Grappi on the footpath *Via di pensa,* was anything but relaxed. He was Guillo Sigliano, Don of the Province of Lazio. A man not accustomed to being told what to do, he scowled as he listened to the message the Monsignor had brought to him from Cardinal Borielli. He shook his head. "What His Eminence asks cannot be done. I cannot kill four foreigners, one of them a woman, in the province of another Don without his consent. No, it is necessary that Don Falzani be consulted. Not to consult him would violate the code of *ricambiare,* His Eminence knows that."

The Monsignor walked slowly, his head bowed, his hands folded in front of him, as if he were saying the Rosary. "His Eminence does not wish anyone to know of this matter until it has been concluded."

Sigliano continued to protest. "But surely, Don Falzani –"

Grappi interrupted him. "His Eminence considers Falzani untrustworthy; he is a young Don with allegiances elsewhere in the Vatican." His voice hardened. "Falzani is not to hear even a rumor of the matter."

The *Via di pensa* ended at a small fountain where a thin stream of water trickled from the grinning mouth of a gargoyle separating two bronze lovers reaching to embrace. Sigliano suggested an alternative. "If the matter can be taken care of here in Lazio, it is as good as done already."

The Monsignor shook his head. "No, it must be done in Tuscany; His Eminence has his reasons."

The Don of Lazio shrugged. "Then there is nothing I can do; I cannot violate *ricambiare.*"

Grappi paused at the fountain. His fingers tested the water trickling from the gargoyle's mouth. "Guillo, how long have you been Don of Lazio?" "I have not counted the years. Why do you ask?"

"It has been twenty years, Guillo. A long time to be Don of the most coveted province in Italy, would you not agree?" A few small beads of sweat appeared on Sigliano's forehead.

He wiped them off with the back of his hand. "I will admit His Eminence has played a role in it, if that is what you are getting at."

Grappi half-smiled. "You understate the case, Guillo. The truth is you have enjoyed your longevity only because of His Eminence, that even today, there are those with influence who would have your body at the bottom of the Tiber if it were not for the favor with which he regards you."

Sigliano's forehead was now covered with beads of sweat. He turned to the Monsignor. "I would not want His Eminence to view me as ungrateful; it is just that –"

Grappi continued to play with the stream of water in the fountain. "I am only the messenger, Don Sigliano; I cannot speak for His Eminence. But I can tell you this." His voice hardened. "I have served His Eminence for many years and have never seen him attach more importance to any matter. His disappointment will be great. So great, I believe, it may cause him to ponder whether you are really the one to be the Don of Lazio."

Sigliano loosened the collar of his shirt. For several minutes he did not say anything. Then he turned to Grappi. "I think you have misunderstood me, Monsignor; I was not saying I would refuse His Eminence's request; I was simply pointing out the difficulties involved."

Grappi smiled. "Of course, of course. You just wanted to be sure His Eminence appreciated the depth of your loyalty; I understand."

The Don of Lazio took a large handkerchief out of his pocket and wiped his forehead. "I will need time to prepare."

Grappi nodded. "Things have been arranged so you will have the time you need." He withdrew his hand from the fountain and shook the water off his fingers. The small drops fell like a blessing on the outstretched arms of the bronze lovers. He turned and started back along the *Via di pensa.* "Come, Guillo, as we walk back I will explain what it is you are to do."

They had only taken a few steps when Grappi put his hand on Sigliano's shoulder, and pointed out across the gardens. "Truly remarkable is it not, Don Sigliano, how all this around us is possible." He smiled. "I mean how it is all made possible by the right use of natural pressure."

Positano, Italy, September 13, 1978 . . . The last thin crescent of the setting sun melted into the Tyrrhenian Sea, turning the whole Bay of Naples into what seemed a vast sea of blood. Then suddenly, the color was gone and it was dusk, the horizon obscured by a descending curtain of darkness.

Alfonso Biancalana watched it all from the balcony of his suite at the elegant Hotel Siranuse in Positano. He turned and looked up at the steep mountain behind him. The lights of the houses perched high above were beginning to twinkle like stars. He was still wearing his bathrobe and slippers. He had tried to take a nap but had just tossed and turned. Beside him on the balcony was a glass table covered with fruit and cheese, none of which he had touched. He was too excited to either sleep or eat. Tomorrow, he was flying to the United States to see

Antonio. He shook his head. It was hard to believe that more than thirty years had passed since he had seen his brother. But it was so. The last time was 1945. He remembered the day like it was yesterday. The war was over but it had left the family's once prosperous olive oil business in shambles. Antonio opted to leave Italy and start a new life in America. He sold his half of the business to Alfonso for a steamship ticket to New York. After Antonio left, Alfonso moved the business to Naples where he used it first as a front in the black market, then later to gain access to the lucrative drug traffic beginning to flourish in southern Italy. Once into narcotics, he discovered that the key to survival was killing, not just one's enemies but if necessary, one's friends, dispassionately, as a matter of business, and always with as much violence as possible. A quick learner, he more than survived, he prospered. In ten years, he was the largest source of heroin south of Rome, by the end of the fifties, the only source. By the time he became Don of Compagna, he had seen as much blood, it seemed, as the sunset had just put in the Tyrrhenian. A cool breeze blew in off the water across the open balcony. He shivered. It was time to go in.

Inside, his Consigliere, a thin dark-skinned Sicilian with a pallid, pockmarked face, was sitting on the edge of a sofa, a small black notebook in his hand. "About time you came in, Don Alfonso; there's a chill in the air. I was starting to worry you'd stay out there too long."

Alfonso dismissed his Consigliere's concern with a shrug. "Have all the arrangements been made?"

The pockmarked face frowned. "Hey, what kind of a Consigliere would I be if you're leaving tomorrow and I hadn't made all the arrangements?" He consulted his black book. "Your plane gets to New York at three; the one for

Boston leaves an hour later. Ligotti's people will have a limo waiting when you get to Boston."

Alfonso took a thick black cigar out of the pocket of his bathrobe. He ran it back and forth across his tongue, and then lit it with a silver lighter. "How far is it to this –" He reached into the pocket of his bathrobe and took out a handwritten letter. He looked through it for the part he wanted. "Ah, here it is; - to this place called Marblehead?"

The Consigliere consulted his black book again. "Less than an hour's drive." He saw that Alfonso was still reading the letter, and settled back on the sofa. He knew Alfonso was going to read it to him again.

"Listen to this, Consigliere. It begins 'Dear Uncle Alfonso.' Hey, this kid of Antonio's is all right! He's never even met me and he calls me 'Uncle Alfonso.'" He poked the letter with his finger. "He says here they're throwing a big party for Antonio and his wife because they've been married thirty years." He waved the letter at the pockmarked face. "Thirty years, Consigliere! What do you say to that, you who cannot keep your prick in the same woman for more than a few months?"

The Consigliere, accustomed to his insults, simply shrugged. "Thirty years is a long time, Don Alfonso."

Alfonso continued to read the letter aloud. "This is the part I like best. He says 'I know you and dad have not been close over the years; that's why it's so important you come.' And get this part: 'If you can't afford the trip, I'll send you the money.'" He stopped reading and wiped his eye with the back of his hand. "This kid of Antonio's, he wants me to come so bad, he says he'll pay my way if I can't afford it!" He laughed. "Me, Don of Compagna, and the kid says he'll pay my way if I can't afford it!" He took out a large red handkerchief, wiped both eyes and then blew his nose. "Okay, I'm going to give myself a shave and a shower. Call downstairs and order me something light." He walked into the bathroom, leaving the door open so he could continue talking. He balanced his cigar on the edge of the sink and began lathering his face. "While I'm shaving, tell me if there's anything else in your black book I should know about."

The Consigliere moved to the edge of the sofa. "There's just one item; it's nothing but a rumor." "What is it?" "Like I said, it's only a rumor. Giamo heard there's a heavy contract out up north; it's coming down in *Valdarno*."

Alfonso stopped shaving. "*Valdarno?*"

"Yeah, I thought it was a funny place too. I asked Giamo if he was sure he heard right. He said he was sure the guy said *Valdarno*."

Alfonso shrugged. "Well that's Don Falzani's province; it's none of our business." He rinsed off his razor. "Giamo say anything else?"

The Consigliere had picked up the phone to call room service. He glanced again at his black book. "Only that it's coming down on orders from the Vatican, and that one of the hits is an American, a woman, the widow of some judge over there."

Marblehead, Massachusetts, September 14, 1978 . . .

It was Regatta Week and Marblehead Harbor was alive with the white triangles of sailboats tacking back and forth, getting ready for the races to begin. The narrow causeway to Marblehead Neck was humming with cars heading out to Chandler Hovey Park, the last point of land on the Neck and the best spot to watch the boats cross the starting line. Once the cars were across the causeway and on the Neck, they would follow a winding road that took them past a point where for fifty yards a high brick wall blocked any view of the surrounding ocean. Behind the wall, perched on a finger of land jutting out into the sea was the home of Antonio Biancalana and his wife, Maria. Antonio had met Maria the second year he was in America, when he was working as an estimator for a large, heavy equipment, construction company in Boston. They were married the next year when Antonio decided to start his own company. The post war years were a boom time for construction work, and Antonio's company quickly grew to almost as large as the one he had left. In the early years, he and Maria liked living in the North End, Boston's crowded but quaint Italian section, but with the growth of his business and the size of their family, they decided to move up the North Shore to the upscale suburb of Marblehead.

Today, as the people driving out to Chandler Hovey Park passed the Biancalana home, they could hear the sound of laughter and the lively strains of tarantellas coming over the brick wall. The Biancalanas were celebrating their thirtieth wedding anniversary with more than a hundred relatives and guests. Even the weather was pitching in. It was a beautiful September day, the sky cloudless, and a soft southwesterly breeze blowing from the land out across the sparkling blue ocean.

Most of the guests were standing, talking, and laughing on the manicured lawn that sloped gently down from the Biancalana house to the rocky beach below. In the middle of the lawn, under a large green and white awning, a string quartet was playing old favorites. A few couples were dancing. On the other side of the house, the asphalt driveway was crammed with teenagers in jeans twisting and jerking to the amplified sounds of a rock band.

Antonio had spent the morning introducing Alfonso to everyone, repeating over and over the story of how they had not seen each other since the end of World War II. It was now after lunch and he was taking his brother for a stroll along the beach. The tide had ebbed and was beginning to come in. They both were enjoying the quiet of being away from the others, and for several minutes they walked together without talking. When they reached the end of the beach and started back toward the house, Alfonso took out two cigars and handed one to his brother. "You know, Tony, you got nice kids; you should be proud of them."

Antonio nodded. "I am. They all went to college and they all got good jobs." He lit the cigar Alfonso had given him. "The only complaint I got is they don't get married; they don't give Maria and me any grandchildren."

Alfonso laughed. "Hey, there's still plenty of time. It's not like the old days; the young people don't get married quick anymore; they want to live together for a while first."

"I suppose you're right." Antonio frowned. "Except for young Joe; he wants to get married real bad. But he's having trouble with the girl friend."

"Oh?" Alfonso was surprised. "He didn't say anything to me about it. I had a long talk with him last night and he didn't say a word about his girl friend."

"He just didn't want to spoil your time here. He knew if he started talking about it, he -" "What's the problem?"

Antonio shook his head. "I don't know the whole story. The girl was married before, to a guy a lot older than her. The guy died about a year ago and, according to Joe, she's all obsessed about digging into his past. She's even going over to Italy where he was during the war. And she won't tell Joe what it's all about. They had a big fight over it."

The wind had shifted, the breeze now blowing in off the ocean had a chill in it. Alfonso picked up a small flat stone and skipped it out over the water. "Hey, don't worry; they'll work it out somehow." He laughed. "I would like to have met this girl of Joe's, though; she sounds like she's got some fire in her. But she's going over to Italy, you say?"

Antonio nodded. "Yeah, and that's really got Joe worked up. The old guy she was married to; he fought over there during the war and she's gone to meet three guys who were in his outfit with him. Joe says they're all getting together because of something that happened in the war, something that's supposed to be a big secret that she won't even tell Joe about. He says there's something screwy about the whole thing and -"

"This thing that happened during the war, where is it supposed to have happened?"

Antonio shook his head. "Joe doesn't know that. He tried to find out but she wouldn't tell him. All he could get out of her was that she was going to meet these three guys and go to some small town in the north somewhere."

Alfonso had picked up another stone and was about to throw it, then stopped. He stood staring out at the water. His brother turned to him. "What's the matter?"

Alfonso shook his head. "Nothing, I was just thinking how your ocean here looks like the Tyrrhenian back home." He turned to his brother. "Tell me something, Antonio."

"What?"

"The old guy, that Joe's girl was married to, the guy that died. What did he do for a living?"

Florence, Italy, September 20, 1978 . . .

Cathy woke up with her face buried in one of the soft pillows on the large queen-sized bed. She opened one eye and saw the message light blinking on the telephone. She was still half asleep and for a moment could not remember where she was. Then she remembered, rolled over and looked up at the ceiling. She smiled. On it was painted a sixteenth century Raphael, another masterpiece seemingly just taken for granted in Florence's elegant Hotel DaVinci. She sat up and looked around the room. It was a mess. Her bags were still unpacked, her stockings and wrinkled suit draped over a chair, everything just as she left it when she climbed into bed a few hours earlier, exhausted by the long flight from Boston. Outside it was dark; she could see the black night through the French Doors that opened to the small balcony overlooking the Piazza del Signoria.

The message light was still blinking. She pulled the telephone into the bed with her, and dialed the *Portinaio*. The voice that answered was surrounded by the noise of the front desk downstairs. *"Buena Sera, Signora?"*

"This is Mrs. Parkman in Room 312. You have a message for me?"

"Si Signora. You had a telephone call from a *Signore* Osterbeek in Suite 434. He would like you to call him back."

"Thank you. Will you connect me to his room now, please?"

"Si, Signora."

Cathy waited. She heard the phone ring twice. Then, on the third ring, a man's voice answered. *"Goeden avond?"* "Mr. Osterbeek?"

"Yes, is this you, Mrs. Parkman?" "Yes, I just woke up."

"You had a long flight. If you would like to rest some more-"

"No, I feel fine now. What's the plan?"

"We are all here in my suite. When can you join us?"

"As soon as I shower and dress."

Osterbeek was smiling as he opened the door. He shook Cathy's hand and drew her into the room. "It is nice to see you again. I hope your flight was not too tiring." He led her into the sitting room of his suite. "Let me introduce you to Cecil Lancaster and Pierre Mollet, two other old comrades of your late husband."

Lancaster shook her hand. "It's a pleasure to meet you, Mrs. Parkman. I trust Jan has told you how much we appreciate your joining us in this endeavor. We're not at all sure we could have done it without you." He glanced at Mollet. "Are we, Pierre?"

Mollet nodded as he shook Cathy's hand. "It would have been difficult. But we are very glad to have you with us, *Madame.*"

Cathy smiled. "I wish you would all just call me Cathy."

Osterbeek motioned for everyone to sit down. "We should get started; there is much to do." He unrolled a large diagram and laid it on the floor where they could all see it. "Here is a layout I prepared of the abbey. I have drawn a circle on it showing where the monks' dormitory and the wine cellar under it were located when the Germans blew them up." He pointed to a pencil sketch beside the circle. "I drew that sketch to show the size and contour of the pile of rubble that is there now." He leaned over and traced his finger along the lines of the sketch. "As you can see, the pile of rubble, several feet high at what was the middle of the dormitory, drops off sharply to only a small amount of rubble where the dormitory ended next to the abbey, where the stone steps led down to the wine cellar, and where we will have to dig to get to the door of the crypt." He turned to Mollet. "Tomorrow night, as soon as it is dark, you and I will go there and begin the digging. By midnight when the sky will be moonlit, we will have the hole dug." He turned to Lancaster. "Cecil, you and Mrs. Parkman-"

Cathy interrupted him. "- Cathy."

Osterbeek smiled. "Yes, of course - Cathy. You and Cecil will remain here at the hotel until ten o'clock; then you will leave to join us. It's about an hour and a half's drive, so you should arrive just when we are finishing."

He hunkered down and pointed to the circle on the drawing. "Here is where Pierre and I will have dug the hole, and where we will all meet. Pierre will be down in the hole to be near the door to the crypt when it opens. He looked at Lancaster. "Cecil, you will remain at the top of the hole while Cathy and I go into the abbey." He pointed to another part of the diagram.

"Here, there is a small door at the back of the abbey we will use to get in. When we get up to the chapel, I will position myself at one of the windows and Cathy will play the organ. As soon as the door to the crypt opens, Cecil will signal me with his flashlight. When I see his signal, Cathy will stop playing." He sat back in his chair. "When we have the document, Cecil and Cathy will take it and leave. Pierre and I will remain behind to fill in the hole and spread some of the rubble over it. The next morning we will all go separately to the airport. I have booked us all on a flight to Rome connecting with Swissair's flight to Geneva." He paused. "Are there any questions?" There were none; the plan was clear. Osterbeek stood up. "Good." He took out a cigar and lit it. Then he turned to Cathy. "Now, I know you would like to hear more about the experiences we all had together with your husband during the war. It was a long time ago, but Cecil, Pierre and I will be happy to tell you everything we can remember."

Two hours later Cathy decided to call it a night. She thanked Osterbeek and the others for telling her so many things she had always wondered about, and then shook their hands indicating she was ready to leave. Osterbeek walked her to the door. He cautioned her about the next day. "I think it is best that we all go our separate ways tomorrow and avoid being seen together." He smiled. "But Florence is a charming city and I'm sure you will not lack for interesting things to see and do." He opened the door for her. "Until tomorrow night, then."

After Cathy had left, Lancaster was the first to speak. "I don't suppose we really have any other choice, do we?"

Osterbeek shook his head. "No, we all agreed. We cannot risk what the Major's widow might do if she learned the true nature of the document, and that we have lied to her about it." He went over again the reasoning for their decision. "Remember, we have led her to believe that the document involved is a plea from Pope Pius XII to Franco to protect the Spanish Jews from Hitler, and that the Vatican is paying us two million dollars for it because it is valuable evidence that Pius XII was not anti-Semitic, contrary to persistent allegations that he was. She has no idea that the Vatican is paying us ten times that amount because the document is just the opposite, an anti-Semitic agreement between the Pope and Hitler that, if published, would provide harmful support for those allegations. We cannot take the chance she would consider what we are doing as criminal and refuse to go along with it or worse still, decide to report it to the authorities." He paused and looked at Mollet and Lancaster. "Are we all still in agreement?" Both Mollet and Lancaster nodded.

Osterbeek walked over to where the diagram he had drawn was still lying on the floor. He picked it up and lit one corner of it with a match. He waited until it caught fire, and then threw it in the fireplace. It disintegrated into small ephemeral pieces of burnt paper floating up into the darkness of the chimney. He turned to Mollet and Lancaster again. "In just forty-eight hours we will all be multi-millionaires." He paused. "And the only possible evidence against us will be locked in a room that no one can enter, because we will have sealed inside it the only key."

Valdarno,   Italy,   September   21,   1978 . . .
The old priest was a sound sleeper. He did not stir at all when Osterbeek and Mollet drove past his house on their way to the abbey, nor when, a few minutes later, the heavy black Mercedes carrying the four men hired by Sigliano followed. Even when a third car pulled off the road, drove around behind his house and parked, he only rolled over without waking up.

It was not until the small cold circle of steel was pressed against his forehead that he stopped snoring and opened his eyes to find himself looking up the barrel of a large cocked pistol. The next thing he knew he was bound, gagged, and propped up in one of his wooden chairs staring in disbelief at the two men who had invaded his home and were now crouched at the window watching the road outside to the abbey.

The one who had bound and gagged him was a giant of a man, his huge head buried without any discernable neck between two massive shoulders, his gray topcoat stretched tightly across his broad muscular back, his large hands hanging from his sleeves like hairy hams. The other, in stark contrast was thin, almost skeletal. His clothes, all black, looked too big for him. As he turned and spoke to the giant, the light from the window showed his pockmarked face. "Remember, Giamo, as soon as they go by, start the car."

Giamo scratched his large head. "There's something I don't get, Consigliere."

"What don't you get?"

"These four guys we're following, that Sigliano hired for the job, you say two of them are really working for our boss, Don Alfonso, and Sigliano don't even know it?"

The Consigliere returned to watching the road. "Yeah, the Ciccarelli brothers up from Bari. The boss is collecting on an old debt the Don down there owes him."

"But how'd the boss talk Sigliano into taking two guys he don't even know?"

"The boss didn't have to talk him into it."

Giamo frowned. "I still don't get it."

The pockmarked face came as close as it ever did to a smile. "The boss called Sigliano and set up a meeting to talk business. When they met, he just dropped it in the conversation that he'd heard about some heavy action coming down in the north without Falzani being consulted."

"What did Sigliano say?"

"He pretended he didn't know anything about it. The boss said it sounded to him like a violation of *ricambiare*. He said he was no fan of Falzani who was a Vatican ass kisser; he just hoped that whoever had the action was smart enough not to use his own people."

"And Sigliano went for it?"

"Yeah, a couple of days later, he called the boss. He said he needed some extra muscle for a job he had, and could the boss give him a couple of names."

"And the boss gave him the Ciccarellis?"

"Yeah." The Consigliere put up his hand. "Hold it! Here they come." He ducked back from the window as the passing car sent a slice of light through the dark room. "Okay, go start the car." The giant stood up. He motioned over his shoulder toward the bound and gagged priest. "What about him?"

"I'll take care of him." The Consigliere remained crouched at the window until he heard Giamo start the car. Then he stood up and walked over to the old priest, now awake and watching him apprehensively. He put two fingers on the priest's chest and made the sign of the cross. Then, his pockmarked face still expressionless, he took out his Beretta, pressed the silencer against the old man's head, and pulled the trigger.

The way Dante Ciccarelli had it figured, it was a better deal for him and his brother Frankie if the girl showed. It meant they'd each get an extra half a million lire for the job. Slouched in the back seat of the Mercedes parked by the side of the road waiting for Lancaster's car to drive by, Dante was only half listening to the dirty jokes Frankie was swapping with the two Sicilians that Sigliano had borrowed from the Don in Palermo. If the girl didn't show, the job would be just another routine hit. Frankie and him would help waste the three guys at the abbey and then head back to Bari. If she showed, they'd get to take out the Sicilians too. He hoped she showed. He could use the extra lire.

Frankie and the Sicilians stopped talking. They all watched as Lancaster's car drove past. Dante smiled. He saw that the girl was in the car.

Cathy looked at the clock on the dashboard. They were late. It was almost midnight and they were not there yet. For over an hour Lancaster had been following a two lane asphalt road that kept twisting back and forth between the dormant vineyards that stretched endlessly into the moonlight on both sides. Lancaster pointed out over the steering wheel at something in front of them. "There's the old caretaker's house; we're almost to the abbey now." As they passed the house, they could see that it was all in darkness. Lancaster laughed. "The old man has probably been asleep for hours."

They had gone less than another mile when a huge structure loomed out of the darkness over a stone wall on their left. It was the abbey.

Lancaster turned off the asphalt road, drove through a gated opening in the wall, and then followed a road behind it that took them up to the abbey's cloister entrance. He saw where Osterbeek and Mollet had left their car, and parked beside it. He turned off the motor, took a flashlight from the glove compartment, and got out of the car. Cathy joined him and they walked down a foot path that went along the outside of the cloister and around to the back of the abbey. They saw Osterbeek standing at the foot of a pile of rubble. He waited for them to join him.

"We've just finished digging to the floor of the wine cellar." He pointed his flashlight into the hole they had dug. "You can see the stone steps leading down to it. Pierre is behind them where the door to the crypt will open." He motioned to Lancaster. "Right here, where I'm standing now is where you should position yourself so I can see you from the window in the abbey. And remember, as soon as Pierre tells you the door has opened, signal me with your flashlight." He turned to Cathy. "All right, let's you and I go into the abbey."

Giamo drove up to the cloister entrance slowly with the car's headlights turned off. He saw the Mercedes, and parked behind it. He got out of the car, walked over to the Mercedes and poked his flashlight through the open window on the driver's side. The two Sicilians were slumped forward, their faces pressed against the blood-splattered dashboard, dime-sized holes in the backs of their heads. He did not bother to look at their faces. He knew what a soft nosed bullet did on the way out. Even their mothers wouldn't recognize them. He snapped off his flashlight and walked back to the car where the Consigliere was sitting, and told him what he wanted to know. "You were right, Consigliere, the girl is with them."

Dante and Frankie had gotten to where they wanted to be. Both were lying prone behind the concrete base of the monks' memorial cross at the top of the pile of rubble. They had left the two dead Sicilians in the front seat of the car, deciding to stuff them in the trunk of the Mercedes later. After they had tightened the silencers on their Berettas and reloaded them with the soft nose bullets they always used for jobs like this one, they had made their way to the back of the abbey, going through the vineyard to avoid being seen.

Osterbeek had taken Cathy around to the back of the abbey where there was a small wooden door. He pushed the door open and they went inside. Osterbeek snapped on his flashlight. They saw that they were in what was once the kitchen. An old stove was still there, now disconnected, rusty and dirty. Beside it on the wall were wooden shelves covered with thick layers of dust. A large cutting table also covered with dust stood in the middle of the room. The place was cold and damp and had a heavy musty smell. Osterbeek panned with his flashlight around the room. In one corner was a flight of stairs. "Ah! That's what we're looking for. Come on, those stairs should take us up to the chapel." They climbed the stairs and found themselves in what was the sacristy, a narrow corridor now with empty rooms on both sides. Osterbeek pointed to one of the rooms as they passed it. "That was the old Abbot's study." They continued down the corridor until it ended at an arched doorway. It was the way into the chapel. They stopped. Osterbeek shined his flashlight into the darkness of the chapel. At the end of its beam of light was the altar. Beside it was a large ornate organ. Cathy, tingling with excitement, rushed through the arched opening to the organ. She told Osterbeek to hold his flashlight over it so she could see it all. Her eyes widened. It was older than any organ she had ever seen.

She frowned and bit her lip. She was a pianist, not an organist; there was a difference, she reminded herself. She had played the sonata many times but never on an organ. She told Osterbeek to hold his flashlight lower so she could examine it more closely. It had only one keyboard; that was a break. She would have to pump it with her feet to get air into the bellows, but she could handle that. She sat down, pushed the stops in fully to keep the organ as quiet as possible, and positioned her feet on the pedals. She took a deep breath and then began playing.

Lancaster made sure he was standing where he could see Mollet in the bottom of the hole, and also keep an eye on the window in the abbey where Osterbeek would be waiting for the signal that the door to the crypt had opened. He bent over and whispered down to Mollet. "They're in the chapel; I saw a light go by the window up there. It shouldn't be too long now." He stood up, cocked his head and listened. The only sound was the wind rustling through the surrounding vineyards. He continued to listen. Still nothing but the wind. Then he heard it. It was faint but he could hear it; the low mournful sound of the organ. He whispered down into the hole again. "I can hear the organ, Pierre; she's playing it now. Get ready, the door should open at any moment."

Cathy had only played a few notes when her whole body was tingling with excitement. She had played the sonata dozens of times. But it was never like this! All the years of wondering what had happened in Italy during the war. Now she knew! And here she was, in the abbey where Charles and the others had hidden, playing the very organ on which he had learned the strange sonata that he was always so mysterious about. The sonata sounded so different coming from the organ, she thought, the way it would have sounded when Charles played it all those years ago. And she was hearing it that way now for the very first time! As her fingers flew back and forth over the keys, her whole body was tingling more than ever. Her face was flushed and she could feel the perspiration running down her neck and between her breasts. She had to fight the urge to pull out all the stops, and fill the whole abbey with music. She reached the end of the sonata, held down the last cord until the sound faded away, and then let her fingers drop into her lap. The organ went dark as Osterbeek took his flashlight away and ran to the window. He looked out and then turned back to her, his face beaming. "It worked! Lancaster is signaling that the door is open!"

Osterbeek was not the only one watching Lancaster for the signal. The Consigliere and Gaimo were watching him from where they were keeping out of sight behind the closest of the cloister's thick columns. And watching him from even closer were Dante and Frankie at the top of the pile of rubble from which they could see down into the hole where Mollet was standing.

Lancaster gave the thumbs-up sign to Osterbeek and Cathy as they hurried back from the abbey. "Good Show! You did it!" He pointed down the hole. "The door is open now; Pierre is putting a stone against it to keep it open."

Osterbeek nodded. "Good. Now let's go down there and get what we came for." He motioned for Lancaster to go first. The Englishman climbed down the stone steps into the hole. Osterbeek held out his hand to Cathy. "You next. I assume you would like to see where your husband and the rest of us had to hide from the Germans."

Cathy smiled. "Yes, I would."

Osterbeek took her hand, turned on his flashlight and helped her down the stone steps to where Mollet and Lancaster were standing by the open door to the crypt with their flashlights on. Osterbeek waited for them to go into the crypt first. Then, still holding Cathy's hand, he helped her through the open door into the crypt. Cathy gasped at the sight of the hideous skeletons leering out at her from the shallow alcoves along the walls. The first alcove was empty, a pile of bones on the dirt floor in front of it. She stopped; she did not want to go any further. The crypt was not at all like what she expected it would be from Osterbeek's description of it when he visited her back in Brookline. He had not even mentioned the skeletons. That was odd, she thought. She could feel an uneasiness beginning to rise inside her. She watched as Osterbeek and the others rushed to the back of the crypt where an iron chest was resting against the wall. Osterbeek knelt down, lifted its heavy lid, and reached inside. He took out the document they had come for, stuffed it in his jacket, and then stood up. "Now, let's get the hell out of here."

Lancaster and Mollet hurried past Cathy toward the door. As she turned to follow them, Osterbeek stopped her. "Wait." He pointed with his flashlight to the third alcove. "There's something I almost forgot, something that has to do with your husband. It's there, in the third alcove.

Here, take my flashlight. I'll wait here. But hurry, we don't have much time."

Cathy took his flashlight, ran to the third alcove, and looked inside it. She frowned. "I don't see anything. What is it I'm supposed to-?" She turned and saw that Osterbeek was slipping out the door with the others.

She realized what was happening and rushed back toward the door screaming "No! No! Wait!"

It was too late. She was too far from the door to reach it before they could close it on her.

Mollet was the first one out. He knelt down quickly, ready to move the stone away from the door as soon as Lancaster and Osterbeek were out.

Lancaster appeared and Mollet heard what sounded like someone spitting from above. Lancaster crumpled to the ground. Mollet, puzzled, stood up to see what had happened. This gave Dante Ciccarelli the target he was waiting for - another straight head shot. The spitting sound again and Mollet slumped back down against the door. Osterbeek appeared and it was Frankie's turn again. Another spitting sound. The Dutchman's head exploded and his body fell forward on top of Lancaster's. Cathy stumbled out of the crypt, still terrified, her face twisted in horror by what was happening. She was shaking all over, her legs were rubbery, and she could feel herself starting to faint.

The giant Giamo jumped down into the hole and grabbed her, keeping her from falling over the bodies in front of her. He lifted her into his arms and carried her up the stone steps and out of the hole. The Consigliere was waiting with a flashlight and a blanket. He told Giamo to keep holding Cathy, and put the blanket over her shoulders and legs. Then he spoke to her. "Signora, we have come to take you back to your hotel. Remain calm; we will get you there safely." He turned and led the way with his flashlight back down the foot path by the cloister to where Giamo had parked the car. He opened the rear door and held it while Giamo put Cathy, with the blanket around her, on the back seat. Giamo then took the Consigliere's flashlight and headed back up the path by the cloister. The Consigliere stood for a moment looking around. He saw that the space where the Mercedes had been parked was empty. He treated himself to a thin smile. The Ciccerelli brothers were already on their way back to Bari. He opened the door on the driver's side of the car and slipped in behind the wheel. He started the motor and then sat back, waiting for Giamo to return. Back in the hole, Giamo had dragged the bodies of Osterbeek, Lancaster, and Mollet into the crypt, checked their pockets for anything that might identify them, and then pushed the stone door back closing the crypt. He climbed up out of the hole, hurried back down the path to the car, and got in the passenger side of the front seat. He told the Consigliere what he had done, and then added. "None of them had anything in their pockets that would identify them. The only thing I found was a bunch of papers with a ribbon around them in one guy's jacket. I took them and brought them back with me."

The Consigliere nodded. "Good work, Giamo; now let's get out of here." He turned the car around and drove out through the wall gate and back toward Florence.

The moon had set and the drive back to Florence through the pre-dawn darkness seemed an eternity to Cathy. Still trembling and in a cold sweat, she kept huddled under the blanket they had given her, her eyes fixed on the backs of the heads of the two men in the front seat, neither of whom said a word during the whole trip. At last, they finally pulled up in front of the Hotel DaVinci. The Consigliere turned and looked back over the front seat. "Signora, we have brought you back to your hotel." He paused. "But you are still not safe while you remain in Italy. Listen to what I tell you. There is a train later this morning that will take you from Florence to Rome in time to make the Alitalia flight this afternoon to the United States. As soon as you get inside the hotel, go to the Concierge. Tell him to make arrangements for you to be on both the train and the plane." He paused. "And until you are safely back home, do not say anything to anyone about what happened tonight." He turned to Giamo. "Get out and walk with her up to the door of the hotel. When you see that she is safely inside, come back and let's get out of here. Our job is finished. What Don Alfonso wanted done has been done."

Giamo started to get out. The Consigliere reached over and put his hand on the giant's arm. "Oh, one other thing."

Giamo looked back at him. "What?"

"Those papers, whatever they are, that you found on one of the guys - give them to her."

Brookline, Massachusetts, September 24, 1978 . . .

Summer was over. It was now Fall in New England's turn. The trees surrounding the Longwood Tennis Club were getting attired in their colorful foliage, and the air had a noticeable bite to it. The players out on the courts were keeping their sweaters on. Cathy and Joe had not come out to the club to play, just to have lunch on the veranda and talk some more. For both of them it seemed a hundred years ago, the last time they were at the club, when they lost the championship because they were fighting over Cathy's decision to go to Italy. But that was all forgotten now because of what had happened since then.

Yesterday, when Cathy arrived in the International Terminal at Boston's Logan Airport, Biancalana was there, standing in the middle of a sea of people, the only one holding a bouquet of roses. When Cathy saw him, she broke into tears, dropped her bags to the floor and rushed over to him. They threw their arms around each other and, oblivious to the crowd bustling past them, stood hugging and kissing, apologizing and forgiving each for everything, and saying again and again how much they really loved each other. On the drive home from the airport, they had to resist stopping and making love right in the car. When they got to Cathy's they did just that, not even waiting to bring in all of her luggage. They spent the rest of the afternoon and all night making love, talking, and making love again. They decided to get married.

Now sitting on the club's veranda, they were enjoying the intimacy of their shared exhaustion from it all. Biancalana motioned the steward to bring them each another gin and tonic. He reached over and took Cathy's hand in his. For several moments he sat there, looking at her, holding her hand and not saying anything.

Cathy smiled at him. "What are you thinking about, Joe?" He squeezed her hand. "I was thinking again about what you told me yesterday and last night. It was awful what you had to go through. I still have trouble believing it all happened." "I can hardly believe it myself." She looked across the table at him. "But it's over now." She looked directly into his eyes. "I mean it's all really over now, Joe."

Biancalana shook his head. "I still can't figure it all out. When you came out of the crypt, the three guys that you went to the abbey with, who were going to lock you inside the crypt, had all been shot dead by someone and you don't know who it was that saved your life."

Cathy nodded. "That's right."

Biancalana continued to shake his head. "Then two guys you never saw before came and took you to your hotel without saying who they were, why they happened to be at the abbey, or anything else."

"That's right. Except that they did warn me that I was not safe while I was still in Italy, and said I should get out of the country as quickly as I could. They also told me not to say anything to anyone about what had happened at the abbey until I was back in the United States. I think they were concerned about the police."

"So you didn't say anything to anyone?"

"No. I felt I owed them that."

Biancalana leaned back in his chair. "You didn't tell me what happened to the document, the one that you went to the abbey for. What happened to that?" Cathy started to say something when the steward arrived with their drinks. She waited for him to leave, and then answered Biancalana's question. "I think it was the big guy, the one called Giamo, who found it in Osterbeek's jacket after the shooting. He gave it to me when they brought me to the hotel."

"What did you decide to do with it?" "I was too upset to even think about it. All I could think about was getting out of Italy as quickly as I could. When I got inside the hotel, I went straight to the Concierge. I told him I wanted to be on the first train in the morning to Rome, and be on the afternoon Alitalia flight to Boston. He said he would make the necessary arrangements for both, and also for a taxi to take me to the train station. He said that time was of the essence and that I should be all packed and ready to leave for the train station in an hour. He said he would telephone my room when the taxi was at the hotel."

She paused. "I went up to my room, laid out the clothes I was going to wear, and hastily packed everything else. I took a quick hot shower and then got dressed. While I was waiting for the Concierge's call, I saw the document on the chair where I had thrown it when I came in the room. I thought about putting a match to it and burning it in the fireplace. But then I remembered Osterbeek saying how important the document was to the Vatican, how it showed that Pope Pius XII was not anti-Semitic, as he had been accused of being, so I did not think I should destroy it. I didn't know what to do. I just wanted to get rid of it somehow, and not be involved with it anymore."

Biancalana reached over and squeezed her hand. "I don't blame you, I would have felt that same way. What did you finally do with it?" "I ended up putting it in a big envelope that I got from the Concierge, and giving it to him to have delivered to the Vatican. I wrote 'Confidential' on the envelope and addressed it to the Cardinal that Osterbeek had been dealing with, the one named 'Borielli.' I thought he'd know what it was and what to do with it." She paused. "And I didn't want it to fall into the wrong hands."

EPILOGUE

The Vatican, September 28, 1978 . . .

Five days after Cathy's return from Italy Pope John Paul, formerly Archbishop Albino Luiciani of Venice, was found dead, sitting up in bed, still wearing his glasses. It appeared he was the victim of a massive heart attack.

The author is a retired litigation lawyer
and lives in Winthrop, Massachusetts.

Would you like to see your manuscript become a book?

If you are interested in becoming a PublishAmerica author, please submit your manuscript for possible publication to us at:

acquisitions@publishamerica.com

You may also mail in your manuscript to:

**PublishAmerica
PO Box 151
Frederick, MD 21705**

We also offer free graphics for Children's Picture Books!

www.publishamerica.com

CPSIA information can be obtained at www.ICGtesting.com
Printed in the USA
BVOW072034151212

308173BV00002B/25/P